A Whispered W

Brady grabbed the phone. "Hello?"

"Hello, Brady." A girl's voice.

Brady shot to his feet, his heart hammering. It was the same voice. The same girl who'd called him before.

"Who is this?" he demanded. "What do you want?"

"I saw you," she replied. "I saw you with Rosha outside St. Ann's."

It's the girl with the scarred face! Brady realized. *It has to be! Who else could have seen us there?*

"Why have you been following me?" he demanded. "What do you want?"

"I already told you," the girl whispered. "Stay away from Rosha. This is no joke. Stay away from her."

Look for more
heart-stopping stories from

FEAR STREET

The Beginning

Runaway

Secret Admirer

FEAR STREET

THE PERFECT DATE

R.L. STINE

SIMON PULSE
NEW YORK LONDON TORONTO SYDNEY NEW DELHI

This book is a work of fiction. Any references to historical events, real people, or real places are used fictitiously. Other names, characters, places, and events are products of the author's imagination, and any resemblance to actual events or places or persons, living or dead, is entirely coincidental.

SIMON PULSE
An imprint of Simon & Schuster Children's Publishing Division
1230 Avenue of the Americas, New York, New York 10020
First Simon Pulse paperback edition April 1996
This Simon Pulse paperback edition February 2021

Cover designed by Heather Palisi
Interior designed by Tom Daly
The text of this book was set in Excelsior LT Std.
Manufactured in the United States of America
10 9 8 7 6 5 4 3 2
This book has been cataloged with the Library of Congress.
ISBN 978-1-5344-8765-9 (pbk)
ISBN 978-1-4391-2041-5 (eBook)

PROLOGUE

Brady Karlin squinted his brown eyes against the sun's glare and let out a long, piercing whistle. "Perfect," he declared. "Absolute, total perfection!"

"What are you saying?" Sharon Noles called out from behind him.

"Miller Hill!" Brady shouted, gazing down from the top of the ridge in Shadyside Park.

Yesterday, a record-shattering blizzard had roared through Shadyside. The storm downed power lines, froze water pipes, and dumped more than three feet of snow before it finally blew out of town.

But yesterday is over, Brady thought. *No clouds today. And even better—no school!*

And Miller Hill, the steepest sledding hill in the park, was one long slope of ice-crusted, blindingly white snow.

Brady whistled again. He itched to hop onto his sled and soar down to the very bottom.

"Brady, I can't hear you!" Sharon shouted. "What did you say?"

Brady turned and waited while his girlfriend of two months trudged along the ridge toward him. Cute *is the word for Sharon*, he thought. She was short and slender, with saucer-size blue eyes and a button nose in a small, round face.

He couldn't see her face at the moment, though. She kept her head down as she staggered along the ridge through the snow, dragging her sled with one puffy-mittened hand.

Brady could hear her gasping. *Definitely not the outdoor type,* he thought as she finally joined him.

"What . . ." Sharon paused to catch her breath. "What were you saying?" she asked again, adjusting the yellow knit hat on her light brown hair.

"Your nose looks like Rudolph's," he teased.

"*That's* what you were whistling and shouting about?" Her whole face flushed with embarrassment. "My nose?"

Brady quickly leaned over and kissed its ice-cold tip. "Forget about your nose." He took her by the shoulders and turned her so she faced downhill. "Take a look at Miller Hill. Talk about an awesome sledding experience!"

"It looks more like *Killer* Hill to me!" Sharon declared. "It's practically a ski slope, Brady. It's so steep."

"The steeper the better," Brady insisted. "It will be so cool. No one has been on it yet. We'll fly!"

"I'm not so sure I want to fly." Sharon glanced along the ridge toward another hill, which was crowded with sledders. "I think we should go over there."

"To the kiddie hill?" Brady made a face. "That's way too tame."

"But it looks a lot safer," Sharon argued. "There aren't any trees, see? And none of those thorny bushes. Nothing to bump into."

"Nothing except a zillion little kids," Brady replied. "We can have Miller Hill all to ourselves."

Sharon bit her lip.

"Listen, Shar, we aren't going to bump into anything," Brady assured her. "And I'll be right beside you. What can happen?"

As he talked, Brady shoved their sleds into position, the tips poised on the edge of the ridge. "Ready?" he asked, tugging his cap down over his curly, dark hair.

Sharon hung back. "Brady, I really don't want to do this."

"Sure you do!" Brady grabbed her hand and

pulled her to her sled. In seconds they lay side by side, belly down on their old-fashioned Flexible Flyers.

"Brady . . ."

"This is so *cool!*" Brady exclaimed.

He reached over and yanked Sharon's sled forward, then pushed off on his own. "Let's fly!" he cried, laughing as the wind hit his face.

The slope was as fast as Brady had hoped. Faster. Almost immediately a clump of thornbushes loomed in front of him.

Quickly he jerked the steering bar and swerved around it.

Next obstacle, a pine tree. Another hard shove on the bar, and the tree was behind him. Ice chips blew back, stinging Brady's face. Cold wind brought tears to his eyes.

He steered around another tree. Another clump of bushes. Flying. Laughing out loud.

"Brady!"

Sharon's scream blew by as she hurtled past him.

"Brady!"

He narrowed his eyes against the ice and wind.

Sharon was way ahead now. Going faster.

Faster.

She's out of control! Brady realized.

A massive pine stood directly in her path.

"Turn the bar!" Brady shouted. The wind tore the words from his mouth. "Turn or jump off!"

"Bradeee!"

Sharon's sled slammed sideways into the pine tree and flew into the air. It bounced over a clump of twisted thornbushes, then skidded on one runner through a stand of twisted pines.

He could see Sharon cling to it. Could hear her frightened screams.

Brady dived off his sled and rolled into the snow. Gasping for breath, he struggled to his feet.

Sharon tumbled helplessly downward—losing her grip on the sled. Her terror-filled cries grew fainter and fainter.

"Sharon?" Brady plunged down through the snow. "Sharon, you okay? Some ride, huh?"

Silence.

Brady stumbled on. Finally he spotted her.

She lay at the bottom of the hill, sprawled facedown in the snow like a rag doll.

"Sharon?"

No answer.

"Okay, Shar, you were right," Brady admitted with a laugh as he hurried the last few steps. "From now on we'll sled on the kiddie—"

Brady stopped.

Sharon lay motionless.

Weird, Brady thought. *That's weird.*

Her back should have been rising and falling as she breathed.

It didn't.

Brady knelt beside her. "Sharon?" he whispered.

No answer. No movement.

Brady put his hand on her shoulder, took a deep breath, and tugged her onto her back.

"No! *Nooo!*" Brady's scream echoed off the snow-covered hill.

Sharon's face! Her cute, button-nosed face!

Nothing was left of it.

No eyes, no lips. No *face*!

Nothing.

The thorns and metal sled runners had sliced it to red mush.

Nothing remained but a pulpy mass of skin and crushed bone.

A bright red puddle of blood on the crisp white snow.

1

The Following Winter

"Not so fast!"

"What's your problem?" Brady looked up from the steaming hot pizza in the middle of the table. His best friend, Jon Davis, had grabbed hold of his wrist, preventing him from diving into his lunch.

"You don't get a slice, or even a crumb, until you spill," Jon insisted.

"Spill what?" Brady asked.

He tried to keep a straight face. But Brady could feel a smirk spread across his face. He loved teasing his friend this way.

"You know what. Stop being such a jerk," Jon pleaded.

"I have no idea what you're talking about," Brady replied.

"What did you find out about Lisa?"

Brady grinned. "She's crazy about me. Satisfied?"

Jon dropped Brady's wrist with a horrified expression on his face. Just the break Brady needed. He grabbed a slice, folded it in half, and took a huge bite.

"You? *You?*" Jon cried. "It figures! I send you to find out if she likes *me*. And the hottest girl at Shadyside High confesses that she likes you! You make me sick, man. Sick."

Brady smiled with a mouthful of pizza as Jon dropped his head to the table. He covered his face with his arms. All Brady could see was his friend's flaming red hair. Jon let out a heavy sigh of defeat.

"Lighten up," Brady said. "So Lisa is not the girl for you. Someone else will come along. I mean, how about that girl at the counter?"

Jon glanced at the girl behind the cash register. Then he reached for a slice of pizza.

"What do you think of her?" Brady demanded. "Is she a Major Babe or what?"

"She's cute enough," Jon replied. "Not my type."

"Great! Then I'll take her!" Brady joked. "I'll get a free pizza every day!"

Jon didn't answer.

"Okay, okay." Brady sighed. "You're still obsessed with Lisa. But I can't believe you don't think that counter girl is hot."

"I can't believe you're checking out other girls at all," Jon mumbled, pulling cheese off his chin. "I mean, what about Allie?"

Allie Stoner was Brady's current girlfriend. Brady knew she wouldn't like it if she caught him coming on to other girls. *But what Allie doesn't know won't hurt her,* he told himself.

"What about Allie?" Jon repeated, starting on his second slice.

Brady shrugged.

"Hey, what's up with you?" Jon asked. "Don't tell me you're thinking of breaking up with her."

"Not exactly."

"What does that mean?"

Brady shook his head. "I don't know. Things are fine, I guess. Don't get me wrong, I really like Allie. But she's a lot more serious than I am."

"Serious about what?"

"About us," Brady explained.

"So what? She really likes you," Jon told him.

"I know. And I like her. It's just that—" Brady broke off.

"Let me guess," Jon said. "You want to go out with other girls, right?"

"Sure. Why not?" Brady asked. "I mean . . . why not?"

Jon shook his head. "Well, I think you're really

messed up, man. But every girl in Shadyside seems to like you. I don't know why, but—"

"Oh wow, Jon. You're jealous," Brady teased, tossing a balled-up napkin at his friend. "Admit it."

"I do." Jon grinned sheepishly. "I wish I had your problem, man. One girl who's too serious about me—and plenty of others just waiting in line."

"It's tough, all right," Brady agreed, his brown eyes sparkling. "I have to figure out how to deal with Allie."

Allie.

Brady closed his eyes and pictured her. Short with auburn hair. Gray eyes, long lashes. A nice bod. Not spectacular, but not bad, either.

A cute mouth, when she smiled.

If only she wasn't so serious about everything.

Especially about him.

With a sigh Brady opened his eyes and noticed a girl sliding into the booth across from them. He let out a low whistle.

"What?" Jon asked.

"That girl over there!" Brady whispered, tilting his head.

Jon rolled his eyes. "Another one?"

"Not just another one—a *perfect* one!" Brady insisted. "Check her out!"

Jon turned his eyes to the other booth, then back to Brady. "Nice. Real nice."

"Nice? She's *perfect*!" Brady exclaimed. "I mean it, man. She's totally perfect!"

As he watched the girl settle into the booth, Brady's heart began to race. He'd never seen such a beautiful girl in his life.

Silky blond hair, swirling past her shoulders like honey.

Huge eyes in a smooth oval face.

Full red lips, slightly pouty.

And her legs! He'd seen them as she sat down. Wrapped in black, skintight leggings, they went on forever!

"You're drooling, man," Jon joked, waving his hand in front of Brady's face.

Blinking, Brady dragged his gaze away from the girl. "I've got to meet her, Jon!" he whispered. "I've got to talk to that girl!"

"Whoa." Jon frowned across the table. "I admit she's kind of great, Brady. But, *what about Allie*?"

"Who?"

"Allie." Jon shook his head. "Never mind. What are you going to do?"

"I don't know. I can't just walk over there and start talking." Brady eyed the girl again.

She turned her head. Met his gaze. And her

perfect lips curved into a *very* friendly smile.

Brady gulped. "Well, maybe I can!" he said, grinning.

"You're making a big mistake," Jon warned him. "Think of Allie."

Brady ignored him and checked out his reflection in the chrome of the napkin holder. He knew he was good-looking. A narrow face with high, chiseled cheekbones. A dimple in his chin. Wide shoulders on a lean, strong body.

But was he good-looking enough for *her*?

And would she like him?

Only one way to find out, he told himself.

He quickly ran his fingers through his curly, dark hair and checked to make sure no stringy cheese dangled from his teeth.

He slid out of the booth and took a deep breath.

"Wish me luck, man," he murmured to Jon.

Jon grabbed his arm. "Come on, Brady. Forget about this."

"I can't." Brady shook off Jon's hand. "I have to meet her, Jon. I can't explain it—but I have to!"

"I mean it, Brady. If you go over there, you're making a big mistake," Jon warned.

Brady laughed and started across the aisle.

He had no way of knowing how right Jon was.

2

"Hey," Brady said softly.

The girl glanced up and smiled again. Her eyes were green, Brady saw. Blond hair, green eyes—a perfect combination.

"Hello." Her voice was low and husky. "Want to sit down?"

Oh man! This was going better than he had planned! Brady shot Jon a quick smile.

"I don't mean to take you away from your friend," the girl said.

"Huh?" Brady's gaze snapped back to her. "Oh no. You're not taking me away from anything." He quickly slid into the booth. "My name is Brady. Brady Karlin."

"Hi, Brady. I'm Rosha Nelson." She picked up a Styrofoam cup filled almost to the brim with steaming black coffee. Her red lips hovered at the edge of the cup for a second. She drew back. "Way too hot!" she declared, carefully setting the cup down. "It's scalding!"

Brady barely heard the words over the sound of his heartbeat. He had never felt such a strong attraction to any girl before. Pounding heart. Sweaty palms. A grin he couldn't control.

Get a grip, he told himself. *Be cool.*

"So." He cleared his throat. "Do you go to Shadyside High?"

She shook her head. Her blond hair shimmered in the light. "St. Ann's," she told him.

St. Ann's, a private school across town. "That explains it," Brady commented.

"Explains what?" she asked.

"Why I've never seen you around school."

Rosha laughed. "Shadyside High is pretty big. I could have been there all along, and you might not have noticed me."

"I would have noticed you," Brady blurted out, feeling his face go hot. "Definitely."

Rosha's smile just about knocked him sideways.

"Listen, Rosha, I— " Brady stopped. "Rosha," he repeated. "That's a weird name. Nice, I mean, but kind of strange. Is it a family name or something?"

"Hardly." Rosha tossed her hair back and

laughed. "My mother's hooked on romance novels. Before I was born, she was reading one that had a heroine named Rosha. I think it's kind of weird. I'd rather have a regular name."

"No way!" Brady exclaimed. "Rosha is really cool. It . . . it fits you."

"What do you mean?"

"Well, it's special," Brady explained. "Like you."

Rosha's lips curved in another smile. "You think I'm special, Brady?"

Before he could think of an answer that wouldn't make him sound like a complete jerk, Rosha leaned toward him. "I saw you looking at me before."

Brady felt his face get hot again. He was usually really smooth with girls, but with her, he kept blushing every two seconds!

"And guess what?" Rosha continued.

"What?"

"I was looking at you, too," she whispered.

"Yeah?" Brady knew he was grinning like a total fool. But it didn't matter. She'd been watching him, too! This was getting better and better!

Rosha laughed. "Maybe our meeting is fate or something. Do you believe in fate?"

Brady had never given fate a thought in his

life. "You bet," he told her. "Listen, Rosha," he added quickly, "I'd really like to take you out sometime."

Sometime soon, he thought. Very soon—*like in five minutes*.

"Hey—okay," Rosha answered. "I'm free on Saturday. How's that?"

"Saturday's perfect," Brady said. "Why don't you give me your address so— "

"No, wait a sec. I forgot," Rosha interrupted. "My mom works on Saturdays, and I promised I'd do some shopping for her at the mall." She paused, thinking. "Why don't we just meet there? Say, six o'clock?"

Brady nodded eagerly. "Downstairs, at the fountain?"

"Great." Rosha lifted her coffee cup to her beautiful lips. She blew on the steaming liquid and lowered the cup back to the table.

Brady couldn't remove his eyes from Rosha's face. He saw her smile fade. Heard her gasp in horror.

For a second he didn't realize what had happened.

Then the pain hit him.

A searing, sizzling pain.

His hand.

His hand was on fire!

3

"Your hand!" Rosha gasped. "I'm so sorry! I didn't mean to—"

Brady finally realized what had happened. She had spilled coffee on his hand.

The coffee burned like lava on Brady's skin. He sucked in a hissing breath and ground his teeth together to keep from yelling.

"I'm sorry! I'm so sorry!" Rosha repeated. She grabbed a handful of napkins and started wiping his hand off.

Brady gritted his teeth harder and tried not to whimper.

The napkins felt like sandpaper.

The coffee was scalding hot!

"I'm sooo sorry!" Rosha repeated, dabbing at his scorched skin. "I wasn't paying any attention. I'm such a klutz!"

Brady wanted to jump up and down and scream until the pain eased. But he managed to control himself. He carefully slid his hand away. "It's okay, Rosha!" he told her, trying to keep his voice steady.

"It's not okay!" she cried, staring at his hand in horror. "It might blister. You'd better get some ice on it. I feel awful!"

So do I, Brady thought. But he didn't want to show it. He glanced over at Jon, who was watching the scene with a frown. "Don't worry about it," Brady insisted, turning back to Rosha. "Really. It wasn't your fault."

"Yes, it was!" she insisted. "I can't believe I did that!"

"Come on—forget about it. No big deal." Brady blew gingerly on his hand, wincing only a little.

"Are you sure you're okay?" Rosha asked, studying him.

"Sure." He took a couple of deep breaths. The pain had eased. He managed a smile. "Of course I'm okay. It feels better already."

"Your poor hand." Rosha cradled it in her own two hands, careful not to touch the burned part.

Her skin felt cool. Soothing.

Gazing at her face, Brady forgot about the pain. "You've got the magic touch," he told her. "I don't feel a thing now."

The worried look began to leave her eyes. "Well, if you're sure."

"Really. I'm fine. No problem." *Just keep holding my hand,* Brady thought.

"In that case, I've got to get home." Rosha sighed. "You know—homework."

"Yeah, me too," Brady agreed reluctantly. No way would he be able to concentrate on his homework. Or on *anything* ever again.

Until Saturday.

Rosha slid out of the booth and draped her backpack over her shoulder.

Brady stood too. "Hey, don't forget Saturday. The fountain at the mall. Six o'clock."

"How could I forget?" Rosha's green eyes glowed warmly at him. "See you Saturday, Brady. Bye."

"Bye." Brady gazed after her as she left the restaurant.

Even after she'd disappeared, he continued to stare.

"You're drooling again," Jon called from the next booth.

Still in a daze, Brady crossed the aisle and dropped down across from his friend.

Jon leaned over and tapped him on the arm. "Earth to Brady. Come in, Brady!"

Brady finally snapped out of it. "She's perfect," he announced. "She's the most perfect girl I ever saw."

"Yeah, but what about you?" Jon asked.

"I think I'm in love," Brady replied with a grin.

"I was talking about your hand," Jon told him.

Brady glanced down. The skin on the back of his hand had turned an angry-looking red. "No big deal," he insisted. "It's not even blistering."

"Not yet," Jon warned.

"I'll put some ice on it when I get home. Okay, *Mom*?"

"I'm not kidding, man," Jon declared. "You ought to have a doctor check it out. That girl almost charbroiled your hand."

Brady grinned. "I didn't even feel it!"

"Brady!" Allie Stoner cried across the hallway of Shadyside High the next day.

Brady stuffed his English book into his locker and peered around the door at his girlfriend. "Hey, Allie."

"I've been looking for you all—" Allie gasped. "Brady! What happened to your hand?"

"My hand?"

"It's so swollen!" Allie's face filled with concern. "What happened?"

"Oh! Uh, just an accident. I dumped hot coffee on myself." Brady turned back to his locker. "It's no big deal."

Meeting Rosha, though—that *was a big deal.*

Allie leaned against the locker next to Brady's. "Anyway, I've been looking for you all day. I thought I'd see you at lunch, but you weren't in the lunchroom."

"Yeah. I had to skip lunch," Brady explained as he pulled out a notebook. "I needed to get some work done in the bio lab."

True, Brady told himself. But only partly true. He had also wanted to avoid Allie.

"You must be starving, then." Allie shifted her backpack and tucked a strand of smooth auburn hair behind her ear. "Want to go to Pete's and get some pizza?"

"Um, no, I can't," Brady replied quickly. "I really have to get home and study."

Allie's gray eyes widened in surprise. "On Friday afternoon?"

Brady forced a laugh. "I'm kind of behind in a couple of things."

Also true. But mainly, he wanted to be alone.

Alone to think about Rosha.

He pulled out another notebook and glanced at Allie.

Come on, Brady, he ordered himself. *Tell her about tomorrow. Tell her you won't be seeing her after all.*

"Listen, Allie." Brady slammed his locker door shut. "About the basketball game tomorrow night—"

"Oh right. That's why I was looking for you," Allie interrupted. "I need to know what time you're picking me up."

Brady closed his eyes for a second. *Do it, Brady.*

"Brady?"

He opened his eyes. Allie gazed at him expectantly. She wore a short, black skirt over gray tights. A reddish-brown sweater that matched her hair, and a gold locket around her slender neck. She looked great.

But not as great as Rosha.

Nobody compared to Rosha.

"Brady?" Allie repeated. "What's the matter? Did your car break down or something?"

"Uh, no, it's not that," Brady told her. "It's . . . I can't take you to the game, Allie. I'm really sorry, but I have to babysit my cousin."

Definitely lame.

But a lot easier than the truth.

Allie flashed him a surprised look. "I thought your cousin was in ninth grade."

"This is another cousin," Brady said. "Chucky. He's only eight. I guess I never mentioned him. He lives in Old Village."

"Oh." Allie's dark eyebrows drew together in a disappointed frown.

"I'm really sorry, Allie," Brady told her. "I was really pumped about going to the game. But my aunt called last night. She was really in a jam."

"I understand." Allie frowned again. Then she brightened. "I know. How about if I go with you? I don't mind missing the game that much. I'd rather spend time with you."

Brady thought fast. "Me too. But Chucky—my cousin—has the flu. My aunt says he has a really high fever. Plus he's throwing up every half hour."

"Poor kid," Allie murmured.

That's Allie, Brady thought guiltily. *She doesn't suspect that I'm lying. She feels bad about a sick kid. A sick kid who's actually in perfect health and doesn't need a babysitter.*

"So anyway, I can't let you come with me," he told her. "You could get sick."

"You could too," Allie pointed out.

"Yeah, but it doesn't make sense for both of us to take the chance," he insisted.

"I guess not." Allie slumped against the bank of lockers and sighed.

"I'm really sorry," Brady repeated. "Hey—maybe we can do something on Sunday."

"We already are," Allie reminded him. "You and Jon are coming over to my house. We're studying together, remember?"

"Oh yeah." Brady had totally forgotten. "Listen, Allie, I have to get out of here. I'm really sorry about the game. But I'll definitely see you Sunday, okay?"

"Okay."

Brady kissed her quickly, then took off down the hall.

At the corner he glanced back.

Allie waved to him.

Even from this distance he could see the disappointment on her face.

Brady waved back, then turned the corner.

He felt guiltier than ever. *Allie is so nice, and she really cares about you,* he lectured himself. *And you just stood there and lied. How could you do that to her?*

Simple.

I did it because of Rosha.

Brady couldn't help it. He couldn't get Rosha out of his mind since the second he set eyes on her.

He couldn't wait to see her again. He'd never felt this way about a girl in his life.

Not even Sharon.

Sharon had been dead for nearly a year. But Brady still thought about her almost every day.

She had been so sweet, with her big eyes and cute nose. When he thought of her, he always tried to picture her before the sledding accident. But sometimes, especially in his dreams, he'd see her face the way it looked that day.

Her torn, bleeding face. No face at all, really. No face at all.

Brady blinked the image away. He pushed through the school doors and strode outside. A cold wind greeted him. Icy flakes of snow swirled down. He barely felt them.

Sharon and Allie had already disappeared from his mind. All he could think of was Rosha. Only one more day. Only one more day and he'd be with her.

Does Rosha feel this way? he wondered. *Is she counting the hours until we'll be together?*

Will she even show up?

She's so perfect, Brady thought. It seemed impossible that such a perfect girl could be interested in him.

But she said she was watching you, Brady reminded himself.

And she talked about fate.

Fate. Brady had never thought much about it.

Was it really fate that had brought him and Rosha together?

Or was she just teasing him? Just having some fun at his expense?

Will she show up on Saturday? Brady wondered for the thousandth time.

Was she serious? Will she be there?

4

Brady stood by the big fountain on the first floor of the Shadyside Mall. He glanced around nervously at the shoppers rushing by.

He didn't know if Allie had gone to the game without him. But even if she had, some of her friends might show up here and see him. He would have some major explaining to do if word got back to Allie that he was at the mall instead of babysitting.

Rosha is worth the chance, he thought. *I just wish she would get here!*

He checked his watch.

Five minutes to six.

Only thirty seconds had passed since the last time he had checked.

Get a grip, he told himself. *You're acting like a thirteen-year-old geek on his first date.*

He made himself sit down on the flat stone

rim surrounding the fountain. Tried to look cool and casual. Nobody could read his mind, after all. Nobody could hear his heart pounding with excitement.

Excitement and fear.

What if Rosha didn't show? He might never see her again.

Brady stood up, too anxious to sit still. He forced himself not to check his watch. He put one foot on the fountain rim and gazed into the water. Pennies and nickels glittered up at him.

Wishing coins.

Why not? Brady thought, staring at the coins. It can't hurt. He dug into the pocket of his jeans and pulled out a quarter.

I wish . . ., he thought, picturing Rosha's face. *I wish . . .*

"Think it will come true?" a husky voice asked.

Brady spun around. "Rosha!"

She wore a plum-colored jacket and tight black jeans stuffed into soft leather boots. Her full red lips curved into a smile.

"You look great," Brady blurted out, his mouth dry. He dropped the quarter.

It made a sharp cracking sound as it hit the floor.

Rosha bent gracefully and picked it up. "A

quarter? Most people toss pennies," she remarked, handing Brady the coin. "Must be an important wish."

"It was." Brady slipped the quarter back into his pocket and grinned at her. "But I don't need it anymore. I mean, you're here."

"You thought I wouldn't come? I was afraid *you* might not show up," Rosha admitted, laughing.

Brady laughed, too, totally relieved. "How about a movie?" he asked. "That new Brad Pitt film is playing over in Waynesbridge."

Waynesbridge was the town next to Shadyside. Brady felt pretty sure he wouldn't run into any of Allie's friends there.

"Sounds great," Rosha agreed. She tucked her arm through his.

"Wait. Don't you have any bags or anything?" he asked. "I thought you had a bunch of shopping to do for your mom."

Rosha sighed. "Couldn't find what she wanted—and she's super picky. It's better to go home empty-handed than with stuff she doesn't like." She hitched a black leather purse onto her shoulder and squeezed his arm. "Let's go, Brady."

"Anything you say!"

• • •

On the movie screen a terrified woman crept down the hallway of her house. Behind her a door opened silently. A pair of dark, menacing eyes peered out.

Brady jumped as something touched his arm.

"It's just me," Rosha whispered softly. She leaned closer to him. "These scary movies always freak me out."

She slid her hand into his. Their fingers intertwined.

Brady took a deep breath.

Perfect, he thought.

The movie is almost over and so far everything is perfect.

He stared at the screen without seeing it and thought about their drive to Waynesbridge. They had talked from the minute they left the mall. And it was so easy! No long, uncomfortable silences. No stumbling conversation or nervous laughter.

"I feel as if we've known each other forever," Brady had told her.

"Me too," Rosha agreed. "I knew it would be like this. I knew it the minute I saw you."

"You did?"

"Sure." Rosha smiled. "I told you it was fate, didn't I?"

"You really believe that?" Brady asked.

"I know it." Rosha smiled again, tossing her head back. Brady liked the way her long blond hair tumbled around her shoulders like a model's in a shampoo commercial.

He liked her laugh. Her low, throaty voice.

Her green eyes and pouty mouth.

He liked everything about her.

Especially the way she squeezed his hand during the scary parts of the movie.

Brady focused on the screen again. The film had ended. The credits were rolling.

And Rosha still held his hand.

"That was great!" she exclaimed as they edged their way up the crowded aisle. "I love happy endings."

Brady gave her hand a squeeze. "Should we get something to eat?" he asked. "There's a Burger Hut a couple of doors down."

"I wish I could," Rosha told him. "But I really have to get back. I promised my mother I'd be home by ten." She sighed. "I know, it's ridiculous. But whenever I go out with somebody she hasn't met yet, she insists I come home early."

"She doesn't trust me, huh?" Brady asked.

"Not yet. But don't worry. When she meets you, she'll like you." Rosha smiled. "And then we can stay out late."

Brady's disappointment vanished. *Then we can stay out late.*

She really likes me. She really wants to see me again!

Rosha shivered as they stepped outside into the cold night air. Brady put his arm around her shoulders, and she snuggled against him. The wind blew a strand of her hair across his face. It felt like silk.

Rosha shivered again. Brady pulled her closer.

And then he saw the girl.

She stood in the shadows under the theater marquee, staring at him.

Brady wouldn't have given her a second glance, except for her face.

It was the most hideous face he'd ever seen.

Scars, Brady realized with a shudder. *Her entire face is covered with red scars.*

Scars crisscrossed the girl's forehead like railroad tracks. Twisted, ropelike scars almost fused her eyelids shut. Her cheeks and chin wrinkled like shriveled apples.

A web of horrible scars, red in the bright light from the movie theater.

As the girl's eyes stared at him from behind the twisted flesh of her eyelids, Brady shuddered again.

He hurried Rosha away. The girl, following his every step. The fierce glint in her eyes made him uneasy.

Who is she? he wondered.

And why is she staring at me like that?

5

"So? What do you say, Brady?" Rosha asked.

"Huh?" Brady turned his eyes from the scarred girl. "Sorry. I didn't hear you."

"I was telling you what I'd like to do now."

The ugly face faded from Brady's thoughts. Maybe Rosha had changed her mind about going home so soon. "Anything. Name it."

"Well, I really like your car," she told him. "How about letting me drive it back to Shadyside?"

No way! Brady thought as they reached the car.

His *dad's* Oldsmobile Cutlass.

The car his father had let him drive exactly two times, on penalty of death if anything happened to it.

"Besides," Rosha continued, playfully squeezing his arm. "You bought the movie tickets and the popcorn. And you drove us here. It's only fair that I do something."

"No, really, that's okay," Brady protested. "Tonight is my treat, all the way."

"That's sweet, Brady, but I *want* to drive." Rosha ran her hand along the side of the gleaming silver-gray car. "I've always wanted to drive one with turbocharge. I bet it's really powerful."

"Uh, yeah, it is," Brady agreed. "The thing is, it's my dad's car. I practically had to sign my life away to borrow it. I'm not kidding. If I bring it home with even a microscopic scratch on it, he'll go ballistic."

"But I'm a good driver," Rosha argued. "Nothing will happen. Don't you trust me?"

"Of course I trust you, but . . ." Brady shook his head. *Of all the things she could ask for, why did it have to be this?*

"Come on, Brady. The night has been perfect so far." Rosha pouted up at him. "Don't spoil it. Let me drive—please? Besides, you'll be right beside me. What can happen?"

"Rosha, I just—"

"Oh, never mind." She abruptly let go of his arm. "Forget I asked."

"Hey, don't be angry," Brady pleaded.

"I'm not. I understand perfectly." Rosha started pulling on her gloves, not looking at him.

Brady stuck his hands into his pockets. She *was* angry, he could tell. Her voice had a touch of frost in it. Everything had been going so great. Now this. "Rosha . . ."

"Yes?" She kept fiddling with her gloves.

Brady stared at her, desperate for her to smile at him again. To like him. If he told her no, she might decide to find somebody else.

He'd never see her again.

Don't blow this, he told himself. *Let her drive. Dad will never know.*

"You have to understand, Rosha, I wouldn't let just anybody do this," Brady told her. "But you're not just anybody, so . . ." He pulled the car keys from his pocket and dangled them in front of her eyes.

Rosha's gaze shifted from the keys to Brady's face. "You mean it?" she asked. "It's not that big a deal, you know."

"Go ahead. Take the keys," Brady said.

"Well, if you're sure."

"I'm positive."

Rosha snatched the keys and kissed him quickly but firmly on the mouth. "Thanks, Brady. Let's drive!"

Brady's lips tingled from the kiss as he trotted around to the passenger side. With gratitude like that, Rosha could take the wheel any day!

But his nervousness returned the second Rosha revved the engine. Shoving the gearshift into drive, she hit the gas pedal. The rear tires spun. When they finally gripped the road, the car shot out of the parking lot with a screech.

"Just take it easy," Brady pleaded, trying to keep his voice calm. "It snowed yesterday, remember? There might be icy patches."

"No back-seat drivers allowed," Rosha ordered, smoothly rounding the corner. "If I see your foot trying to hit an imaginary brake pedal, you'll have to hitch back to Shadyside."

Brady laughed, hoping she was kidding.

In a couple of minutes they had left the lights of Waynesbridge behind. Ten miles of dark highway stretched ahead of them.

Rosha stomped on the gas pedal and laughed as the car surged forward. "Major horsepower! This is fantastic!"

Brady forced a smile. He swallowed dryly as the white lines on the road zipped beneath them in a blur. *Relax,* he told himself. *It's a straight ten-minute drive. Or a* two-*minute drive, at the rate we're going!*

"We need music!" Rosha cried. She took one hand off the wheel and fumbled for the radio dial.

"You drive," Brady told her quickly. "I'll handle the radio."

"Perfect!"

Brady leaned over and punched the buttons until he found a good station. Loud music filled the car, its heavy beat thudding over the rumble of the engine.

He gazed at Rosha. She had the driver's window open a crack, and a strand of blond hair whipped back in the breeze. She glanced over at him and grinned. Her green eyes glowed with excitement.

"See?" she shouted over the music. "I told you I was a good driver!"

"Right!" *Good and fast,* Brady thought as the car ate up the highway.

Too fast.

A wide patch of ice loomed ahead. Brady's right foot automatically pressed against the floorboard. His hand gripped the armrest.

Rosha glanced at him again. "Lighten up!" she teased. "Remember what I said about hitching home!"

She pressed down harder on the gas pedal. The car flew over the ice.

Brady took a deep breath.

He wished he could see the speedometer. Rosha had to be way past the speed limit. As casually as possible, he glanced over his shoulder. Good, no flashing lights behind them. The last thing he needed was to get pulled over.

He faced front again and saw the exit sign for Shadyside.

The car sped forward. Brady's palms were sweaty and his heart raced.

It's almost over, he told himself. *Be cool. Don't let her see how nervous you are. We'll be off the highway in a minute. She'll have to slow down then.*

The exit sign loomed closer.

Closer.

Rosha took the turn at top speed. Brady slammed against the passenger door as they flew up the exit ramp.

"Slow down!" Brady cried sharply. "Rosha!"

The car roared and picked up speed. The exit ramp curved toward a residential street.

"Hey—come on!" Brady yelled. "There's ice on this ramp! Ease up!"

"I-I'm trying, but I can't!" Rosha cried. Brady could hear panic in her voice. "I can't slow down! The gas pedal—it's stuck!"

"Pump the brake!" Brady shouted.

As Rosha's foot fumbled for the brake, the car skidded onto a patch of ice. It swerved wildly to the right. Rosha yanked the steering wheel to the left.

"Too far!" Brady yelled. "Pull it back!"

Rosha yanked the wheel again—and hit the brake at the same time.

The car spun.

"Brady!" Rosha screamed, pointing straight ahead.

Brady's heart stalled.

He saw a parked car sitting at the end of the street, its rear window shining with frost under the streetlight.

The parked car seemed to grow huge as they hurtled toward it.

"Brady!" Rosha screamed again.

Brady dived for the steering wheel.

Too late!

Metal crunched and glass shattered as they plowed into the back of the parked car. The impact threw Brady forward.

I'm not stopping, Brady realized.

No seat belt.

I'm dead!

Brady screamed in terror. And shot headfirst into the windshield.

6

A drumbeat pounded. Throbbing.

Loud.

Painful.

Brady groaned.

Something took hold of his shoulder. Shook him.

He groaned again.

"Brady!" a voice cried frantically in his ear. "Brady, wake up!"

Rosha's voice. Urgent. Frightened.

Rosha's hand, shaking him.

Brady forced his eyes open. Lights. A blur of motion.

"Brady, come on!"

Slowly Brady's vision cleared. He gazed at the windshield of his father's car.

An intricate spiderweb of cracks spread out over what used to be smooth, clear glass.

Brady blinked, trying to figure it out. "What happened?" he mumbled.

"We crashed into a car!" Rosha whispered in his ear. Her fingers dug into his shoulder. She shook him again. "Wake up now. You have to wake up!"

Pain stabbed through Brady's head as Rosha shook him. He reached up and touched his forehead. Something wet and sticky came off on his fingers. Blood.

Brady took a shaky breath and slowly began to remember what had happened. Rosha driving too fast. The ice. The parked car, looming in front of them. And then that horrifying crash into the windshield.

No wonder his head hurt. He touched it again. Felt more blood. Dizziness swept over him.

"Brady!" Rosha breathlessly repeated his name.

He turned and focused on her worried face. "I guess I blacked out for a second," he murmured. "You okay, Rosha?"

"I'm fine. Brady, listen to me!" Rosha cried, tugging on his shoulder. "We have to switch places!"

"Huh?"

"You have to switch places with me!" Rosha's voice rose frantically. "I don't have a driver's license!"

"You don't . . ."

". . . have a license!" Rosha repeated. "People are coming out of their houses, and the police will be here any second! We've got to switch seats!"

Pain stabbed at Brady's head again. Music still blared from the speakers. *At least the radio isn't broken,* he thought. But the music hurt his head. He reached out and shut it off.

"Would you forget about the music? You have to move!" Rosha tugged at him, harder. His head throbbed, but she didn't stop. Finally she climbed over him, then shoved him over the gearshift and into the driver's seat.

"I'm so sorry!" she cried. "I feel totally awful about this, Brady. But I can't get caught driving without a license. Please say you understand!"

"Sure." Through his daze, Brady could hear a siren wailing in the distance. "You sure you're all right, Rosha?"

"Yes! Really, I don't have a single scratch." She leaned over and kissed his cheek. "I'm really, really sorry about this, Brady!"

"Don't worry," he murmured. "Everything will be okay."

The siren grew louder. Brady straightened up. *Seat belt,* he thought. *Don't want to get a ticket for not wearing a seat belt.* He snapped it in place and the movement made his head throb. He touched his face gingerly.

An egg-size bump near his hairline. And a cut, still seeping blood.

The siren whooped loudly, then cut off. A car door slammed. Footsteps crunched on the frosty road.

Brady rolled down the window and gulped in the cold air.

A flashlight blinded him for a second. Then a police officer poked his head in the window. "You okay, son?" he asked in a gruff voice.

"Yeah, I think so." Brady tried to sound alert. "There's a patch of ice on that exit ramp. The car just hit it wrong, I guess."

"Lousy road conditions all over the place," the policeman agreed. He flashed his light into the interior of the car. "You alone in there?"

"Alone? No, I . . . we . . ." Brady turned toward the passenger seat.

Empty.

Rosha was gone.

7

"You're one lucky dude, Brady," Jon said the next afternoon as he and Brady walked up the driveway to Allie's house. "And you're not even grounded," he added. "If I totaled *my* father's car, I wouldn't see the outside world again until I was twenty-five."

"It's not totaled," Brady corrected him. "It just needs a new windshield and some work on the front bumper."

"Just?" Jon shook his head in disbelief. "Don't tell me your dad didn't freak."

Brady winced, remembering the look on his father's face when he heard about the car. "Oh yeah. He freaked, all right. If I didn't already have this lump on my head, he probably would have put one there."

"I don't suppose you told him who was really driving," Jon said softly.

"Are you kidding?" Brady shook his head. "I don't have a death wish, you know."

"Could have fooled me. I mean, you let this girl drive," Jon reminded him. "She wrecks the car and lands you in the emergency room. Then she takes off."

"I told you, she was scared because she didn't have a license." Brady felt defensive. "And her name is Rosha, not 'this girl,' okay?"

"Okay, okay." Jon climbed the front steps of Allie's house and reached for the doorbell.

Brady grabbed his arm. "Don't forget—Allie thinks I was babysitting last night," he reminded Jon in a low voice. "She called me this morning, so I told her about the accident. But she doesn't know about Rosha."

"This really stinks," Jon said. "I mean, Allie is my friend, you know. Why don't you just break up with her instead of doing this?"

"I will, once I figure out how to tell her," Brady promised. "I just don't want her to find out by accident, okay?"

"Okay," Jon agreed reluctantly. "But if you're so worried about her finding out, how come you told her you'd come over today? You know she's going to have a zillion questions."

"Yeah, but it's better than hanging out at

home," Brady replied. "I'm not exactly Mr. Popularity there at the moment. Anyway, don't mention Rosha."

Brady stabbed the doorbell with his finger. Allie opened the door almost immediately. Her eyes widened as she stared at him.

"Your head!" she cried. "Oh wow!"

"Yeah, he's the walking wounded, all right," Jon muttered. "But don't waste your sympathy on him, Allie. He's not even grounded."

Allie stared at Brady's bandaged head.

"I'm fine, Allie," Brady insisted. He dumped his books on the floor and took off his jacket. He slowly lowered himself to the flowered couch in Allie's wood-paneled family room. His head throbbed.

"But you *do* have to pay for the repairs, right?" Jon asked, stretching out on the rug in front of the fireplace.

"Worse," Brady told him. "The insurance will definitely go up, and I have to pay the extra. I think I should start looking for a job."

Jon groaned sympathetically. "I'll ask at The Doughnut Hole," he offered. "Maybe they need somebody else to work a couple of hours after school. At least we'd get to work together."

Allie shook her head. "I can't believe you guys are talking about money. Brady could have died!"

"Yeah, well, I didn't," Brady reminded her.

"He just *looks* like he did!" Jon joked.

Allie shook her head again and curled up on the couch next to Brady. "How come you borrowed your father's car, anyway?" she asked. "You've only taken me out in it once. It's kind of fancy just to go babysitting, isn't it?"

"Uh, yeah." Brady shifted uncomfortably as he felt Allie's gray eyes boring into his. "A couple of the tires on my car are kind of worn. I thought Dad's car would handle the ice better. Guess I was wrong."

Brady exchanged a glance with Jon. He knew Jon thought he was crazy.

Crazy to let Rosha drive.

Crazy to be sneaking around on Allie.

He had promised to keep his mouth shut about it, though. And Brady knew he could trust him.

But coming to Allie's house had been a mistake. Not because his head still hurt. But because he had to face Allie and lie to her.

Again.

He didn't want to keep talking about it.

Lying about it.

His head began throbbing again.

"Are you okay?" Allie murmured anxiously. "Do you want some aspirin or something?"

"No. Thanks," he told her.

"How's your cousin?" she asked.

"Which one?"

Allie flashed him a confused look. "The one you were babysitting. You told me he had the flu, remember? He's throwing up all the time?"

"Oh. Right. Chucky. He's . . . getting better." Brady shot another glance at Jon. *Help me out, here, man.*

"You know what's missing?" Jon scrambled up from the rug. "Music! This place is as quiet as a tomb."

"Music would be great," Brady agreed. "Crank it up." So Allie can't ask me any more questions.

Jon said, "Alexa, play Billie Eilish." In seconds her voice filled the room. "Come on, Allie, dance with me before we hit the books!" Jon yelled, pulling her off the couch.

Allie laughed and the two began dancing in the middle of the big family room.

Brady closed his eyes, relieved. He could always count on Jon. Allie loved to dance. As long as the music kept playing, she would forget about everything else.

And he could think about Rosha.

Was she all right?

Why had she disappeared like that?

Brady frowned. She must have run because she was afraid of getting caught without a license. It freaked Brady out whenever he thought of it. If he had known, he would never have let her drive his dad's car! Rosha shouldn't even have asked in the first place. If it were anyone else, he would be furious.

But it wasn't anyone else. It was Rosha.

He couldn't be furious with her. So she didn't have a license. Brady was in the driver's seat by the time that cop arrived. No way could he know that Rosha had been driving.

Brady shifted on the couch, his head pounding.

Maybe Rosha just freaked. Or maybe she had some other reason for leaving. Something he didn't know about.

If only he could talk to her. If only he had her phone number! All he could do now was hope that she would call him.

Brady slumped deeper into the couch. He had to find her. Talk to her. Be near her.

He couldn't get her out of his mind.

The music ended. Allie flopped down on the couch beside Brady.

"I'm dying of thirst," Jon announced. "Allie, got any Cokes?"

"Plenty. Get some for me and Brady, too." Allie

touched Brady's shoulder. "Or would you rather have hot chocolate?" she asked him. "Or something to eat?"

"Coke is fine." Brady glanced at her as Jon left the room. Allie's cheeks were flushed from dancing and her eyes sparkled.

She's so pretty, Brady thought.

But she's not Rosha Nelson.

Nelson. You know her last name, you moron! Brady told himself. *Look it up in the phone book!*

A crackling, crunching sound burst from the kitchen. "Whoa!" Jon's voice cried. "Major disaster with the nacho chips in here!"

Allie laughed and scooted off the couch. "I'll go see what happened. Be right back."

As soon as Allie was out of sight, Brady shot across the room to the telephone. It sat on a low table with a shelf beneath it. He grabbed the phone book off the shelf and turned to the N's.

Needham . . . Neldin . . . Nelson!

Brady's heart sank. The name Nelson took up almost three columns.

And he didn't know Rosha's father's name. Or her mother's. Or her address.

Frustrated, he shoved the book onto the shelf and returned to the couch. He started to sit, then changed his mind and strode to the kitchen door.

He couldn't just sit here when Rosha was out there, somewhere. . . .

Allie held a dustpan while Jon swept nacho chips into it. "Hey, guys, I think I'll go home," Brady announced. "My head is killing me."

Allie hurried to his side. "I bet it was the music. Why don't I give you some aspirin and then we'll study the way we planned," she suggested.

"Thanks, but I wouldn't be able to concentrate."

"Oh. Okay, let me get my car keys and I'll— "

"No," Brady interrupted. "I'll walk, Allie. The fresh air will probably help."

"Yeah, let him air his brain out." Jon stuffed some chips into his mouth and gave Brady a sharp look.

Brady ignored it. He gave Allie a quick kiss, grabbed his jacket and books, and hurried outside.

He lived only four blocks away from Allie. They both lived in the North Hills section of Shadyside.

Where did Rosha live?

When would he see her again?

Brady gulped in deep breaths of the chilly air.

Would he see her again?

I have to, he thought. *I have to!*

He crossed the street and turned the corner. Two more blocks and he'd be home.

But then what?

Get a grip, he scolded himself. *Call every Nelson in the phone book until you get the right one. It might take forever—but you'll find her.*

You have to.

Brady hurried down the last half block and turned into his driveway. As he strode toward his house, he heard a car pull in behind him.

He turned quickly, hoping it might be Rosha.

And saw a police car.

The black-and-white cruiser coasted to a stop. At the wheel sat the same cop from last night.

A chill of dread crept up Brady's spine. His heart started hammering.

Did they find out I wasn't driving?

Brady took a deep breath.

If the cops had found out he'd lied, he was in trouble.

And so was Rosha.

Major trouble.

He forced a smile and approached the cruiser.

8

"Afternoon." The officer Brady had met yesterday climbed out of the car. "How's the head, son?"

"Not too great." *Act like you're still hurting,* Brady told himself. *Maybe he will go easy on you.* "I was trying to study," he added, hefting his notebooks. "It's a little hard to concentrate, though. Feels like somebody is using my head for drum practice."

The officer nodded, a serious expression on his face. "Hope you feel better soon."

Why? Brady wondered with a flash of panic. *So they can question me?* "Thanks," he replied. "It's not too bad."

The officer cracked a smile. "Yeah, you look like you've got a hard head." A growling sound came from his throat.

Brady realized the cop was laughing. He

swallowed again and managed to chuckle along. If this guy was playing some kind of game, he wished he'd get it over with. "Listen," he said. "I really should get inside and try to do a little homework."

"Well, to tell you the truth, I didn't drop by just to ask about your head," the policeman told him. "Got another reason."

Brady tensed up. Here it comes. "Oh?"

The officer turned and leaned into the open window of the cruiser. "We found something in your car when it was towed away," he said, speaking over his shoulder. "Thought you might be interested in it."

What? Brady wondered. *What could they have found that would prove he wasn't driving?*

The officer straightened up and turned around. "This was under the front seat. Ever seen it?" he asked. He held a black leather pocketbook with a long, thin strap.

Brady stared at it.

Rosha's bag. She must have tossed it onto the seat when she got in to drive. Then it fell during the crash.

Rosha's bag! And inside would be her wallet. Some ID. Her phone number or at least her address.

"Sure I've seen it," he told the policeman. "It's my girlfriend's. She thought she lost it on our last date."

"Must have been wedged under the seat all this time," the cop said, handing the bag to Brady. "She'll be happy to see it."

"She sure will. Hey, thanks. Thanks a lot!"

"You bet. Take care of that head now." The officer climbed into the car and backed it down the driveway.

Brady gave him a quick wave, then hurried up the driveway and let himself into the house. He dumped his books on the hall table and started to open the bag.

"What's that, Brady?" his mother asked, trotting down the stairs with a stack of bath towels in her arms.

"Huh? Oh." Brady stuck the pocketbook under his arm. "It's Allie's purse."

"Oh?"

"The police brought it by," Brady explained. "They found it in Dad's car."

"In your father's car?" Mrs. Karlin blew a strand of dark hair off her forehead and frowned. "Allie wasn't with you last night, was she?"

"No," Brady replied quickly. "I took her out in his car once before, remember? I guess she left it then."

"Well, you should let her know," his mother advised. "I'm sure she spent a lot of time looking for it."

"Yeah, I'll do that right now." Brady took the stairs two at a time.

Up in his room he shut the door and tossed his books on the desk. Then he crossed to the bed and sat down, the telephone in easy reach on the nightstand.

Soon he would be in touch with Rosha.

He would hear her throaty voice.

Maybe they would see each other tonight.

Eagerly he unzipped the bag and pulled it open.

And gasped in shock.

9

The bag was empty.

Had someone stolen all the stuff out of it?

Brady pulled the bag open as wide as it would go and stuck his hand inside.

Nothing. Not a stray penny or a scrap of paper. Not even any lint.

He turned the pocketbook upside down and shook it.

Nothing fell out.

No one would steal every last thing from a bag, would they? Besides, the cop had said it was wedged under the seat. Who would go through a purse and then stuff it back under a car seat?

Brady tossed the bag aside and slumped back against the headboard.

Weird.

Why would Rosha carry around a completely

empty bag? She had been shopping for her mother. Who went shopping without money or a credit card? Maybe she kept her wallet in her jacket pocket or something, so if the bag got snatched, she'd still have her money.

Brady shook his head. That didn't make any sense. Why carry the bag at all?

You're back where you started, he told himself. *No phone number. No address.*

Sighing, Brady slid off the bed and paced around the room. He stopped at the window and stared out at the gray day.

Where are you, Rosha? Why did you run away? Why haven't you called me?

He turned from the window and started for the door. His parents kept a phone book in their room. It was time to start calling all the Nelsons in Shadyside.

As he put his hand on the doorknob, his telephone rang.

Rosha?

Brady leaped for the phone and snatched it up in the middle of the second ring. "Hello?"

"Hi, are you feeling better?"

Allie.

Brady's shoulders sagged in disappointment. "Hi, Allie. Yeah, I'm fine now."

"Really?" Allie's voice was doubtful. "You were so pale before. And the way you took off—I was really worried."

"Don't be," he told her. "I said I'm fine. Everything's great."

Or it will be, he thought, *as soon as I find Rosha.*

"Are you sure?" Allie asked. "You sound weird."

Right, Brady thought. *Weirdly, incredibly crazy about a girl I can't even find! And I have to find her. I have to see her again.*

"Brady, did you hear me?" Allie asked. "I said you sound really weird."

"I'm here," he replied. "Sorry, Allie. I'm a little wiped. That's why I sound strange, I guess."

"Maybe you should call the doctor," she suggested. "Or at least lie down for a while."

"Lie down—that's a good idea," he said quickly. "I think I'll do that right now."

"Okay, I'll only keep you a minute," she promised. "I just wanted to say I copied over the notes for you when Jon and I were studying. I'll give them to you tomorrow, okay?"

"Sure. Great." Brady glanced impatiently at the door. He couldn't think about notes or studying now. He just wanted to get that phone book and get started finding Rosha. "Thanks, Allie. I'll see you at—"

"Oh, one more thing," she interrupted. "About Saturday night."

Brady tensed. *What did Allie know about last night? Had Jon told her about Rosha?* "Saturday?" he asked, trying to sound calm. "What do you mean?"

"Next Saturday, remember? At Mei's?"

Next Saturday. Not last night. Brady sighed with relief.

But then his mind went blank. Mei? The only name on his mind at the moment was Rosha. He forced himself to concentrate. Mei, Mei . . . Mei Kamata. Right, one of Allie's friends.

"Brady, are you there?" Allie asked sharply.

"Sure. What about Mei?"

"She's having a party next Saturday night," Allie reminded him. "And we're invited."

"We are?"

"Brady, I told you about it last week!" Allie cried. "Are you sure you're not really sick? That bump on your head . . ."

Brady sat on the bed. *Get it together, man,* he ordered himself. "Sorry, Allie. I'm just tired. Sure, I remember the party."

"Okay. Anyway, it was going to be just a regular party, you know?" Allie continued. "Music and food and like that. But then she remembered—there's a vacant lot at the end of her block, and every winter the neighbors flood it and it freezes over."

"And?" Brady tapped his foot.

"And everybody ice-skates," Allie said. "So Mei decided to have an ice-skating party."

"That sounds cool." *She could have told me this at school,* Brady thought. *The party is almost a week away.*

"Good. You do have ice skates, right?" Allie asked.

"Sure." Somewhere. "I'll dig them out."

"Brady . . ." Allie hesitated. "You sound a million miles away. Is something on your mind?"

Rosha is on my mind, Brady thought. *My mind is wherever she is.* "I just can't concentrate right now," he told Allie. "I think I'll lie down."

"Wow. Your poor head!" Allie cried. "Take it easy, Brady. See you tomorrow."

"Tomorrow. Bye, Allie." Brady slammed the phone down and hurried across the hall to his parents' room for the telephone book.

Back in his room he shut the door again and sat on his bed, the telephone on his lap and the open phone book beside him.

Nelson, A., on Melinda Lane was the first entry.

Brady dialed the number and got an answering machine. He hung up. He hadn't thought about leaving a message. If it wasn't Rosha's place, they would ignore it.

He penciled a question mark next to Nelson, A., and went to the next entry.

He let the phone ring ten times, then hung up.

A man answered the third call. "Uh, hi. Is Rosha there?" Brady asked.

"Who?" the man demanded loudly. "Joshua, did you say?"

"No. Rosha," Brady repeated.

"Nobody here by that name," the man declared. "No Joshua, either." He hung up.

This could take forever, Brady thought.

But it's worth it, he told himself. *Finding Rosha is worth anything.*

Brady ran his finger down the page and found the next number. As he started to pick up the phone, it rang.

He tightened his grip on the receiver for a moment. Rosha?

No, probably Allie. She always forgot to tell him things. Always had to call back once or twice. This was probably more about Mei's party.

Still, his heart raced as he picked up the phone. He could be wrong. It could be Rosha. "Hello?"

Silence. But he could hear someone breathing. "Hello?" he repeated.

"Brady."

A girl's voice.

But not Allie's. Not Rosha's, either. He didn't recognize it.

"Who is this?" Brady demanded. "Hello?"

"I'm here, Brady," the girl replied. "And I've got a message for you."

"Who is this?" Brady repeated.

"Stay away from Rosha," the girl whispered.

"Excuse me?" Brady sat up straight. "Is this some kind of joke?"

"It's not a joke, Brady." The girl's voice hardened. "It's a warning. Stay away from Rosha."

"Who is this?" Brady demanded again. "A friend of Allie's? Who *are* you?"

The phone clicked.

Silence. Then a dial tone.

10

Brady rushed to his locker after school the next day, eager to get out. He yanked his jacket off the hook and quickly shrugged it on as he hurried down the crowded hallway.

"Brady, wait up!"

Hearing Allie's voice, Brady groaned. The last thing he wanted right now was to talk to Allie.

He glanced over his shoulder and saw her at the far end of the hall, threading her way toward him through a knot of kids. With another soft groan he stepped out of the flow and leaned against some lockers.

He watched Allie's face as he waited for her to catch up. Smiling, just the way she had been at lunch. Nothing in her expression to make him think she knew about Rosha.

But that strange caller warning him to stay

away from Rosha—she had to be one of Allie's friends. She just hadn't told Allie.

Not yet, anyway.

"Oh wow. What a long day," Allie groaned as she finally reached Brady's side. "I can't wait to get out of here."

"Yeah, me too," Brady agreed, eyeing the doors that led to the student parking lot.

"I know. Let's go buy a bunch of junk food," Allie suggested. "Then go to my house and study for the bio midterm together."

Brady shook his head. "I can't, Allie."

"Why not? You've been worrying about bio for weeks," she reminded him. "Oh, wait—is your head hurting again?"

"No, but I've . . ." Brady thought fast. "I've got to find a job, remember? So I want to get home and take a look at the help-wanted ads in the paper."

Lame, he thought. *Really lame.* He wished he were a better liar.

Allie frowned. "Why don't you go to the guidance office instead? They have all kinds of job listings for Shadyside kids."

"I already tried them," Brady lied. "All they have are babysitting and snow-shoveling. I want something that will pay better."

"Oh. Well, you can look at the paper at my house, you know," Allie told him.

Why won't she just let me get out of here? Brady wondered. "I know, but I better get home," he said. "My mom gave me a ton of chores to do—part of the punishment for wrecking the car."

"Okay. I'll see you tomorrow, Brady." Allie's smile was sympathetic.

And disappointed.

As Brady left her standing in the hall, he felt a twinge of guilt. Should he have told her about Rosha and gotten it over with?

No. Not yet. He had to find Rosha first. Make sure everything was all right between them. Then he'd break the news to Allie.

But how? How was he going to find Rosha? He had called at least twenty Nelsons yesterday and struck out with all of them. All he could think of to do was go home and try some more.

Eager to get home and start phoning, Brady slammed out the door. As he strode toward the student parking lot, he suddenly remembered something.

Rosha went to St. Ann's.

She had told him that the day they met at Pete's Pizza.

Brady felt a smile spread across his face. He

had dated a girl from St. Ann's before. He remembered waiting for her after school.

St. Ann's let out half an hour later than Shadyside High.

In ten minutes Brady could be over there, parked across the street.

Waiting for Rosha.

As he hurried through the rows of parked cars, Brady caught a glimpse of Jon's red hair a few rows away. "Jon, hey!" he yelled. "Hold it a second!"

Jon waved.

Brady ran up to him. "I'm glad I saw you," he declared breathlessly. "I need your help."

"Sure. What's up?" Jon asked.

"We're going to St. Ann's to look for Rosha," Brady explained, grabbing Jon by the arm and pulling him toward his car. "I'll stake out the front and you park in the back. That way one of us will see her for sure."

"Whoa." Jon stopped walking. "I can't go to St. Ann's now. I have to be at The Doughnut Hole in twenty minutes. Besides . . ."

"Twenty minutes is plenty of time—if we leave now," Brady insisted. "Come on, let's get going!"

Jon didn't move. "This is crazy."

Brady stared at him. "What are you *talking* about? You know how I feel about Rosha."

"Yeah, but I don't understand why," Jon declared.

"You don't have to understand!" Brady almost shouted. "All you have to do is help me out!" He grabbed the front of Jon's jacket and pulled. "Come on, man. Move!"

"Get it together, Brady!" Jon peeled Brady's fingers loose, then shoved him away. "You're totally losing it! Lying to Allie, wrecking your dad's car, staking out St. Ann's. Stop acting like an obsessed jerk. She's just a girl!"

Brady angrily jabbed his fingers into Jon's chest. "You don't know what you're talking about!" He jabbed at him again.

Jon rocked back on his heels. His friendly, open expression turned dark and angry. He shot a hand out and grabbed Brady's wrist. "Better get going, Brady," he muttered through clenched teeth. "You might miss her if you spend time fighting with me!"

With a final disgusted glance, Jon flung Brady's hand away and strode off through the parking lot.

Brady spun around and jogged angrily to his car. He revved the engine, then peeled out of the parking lot in a spray of ice and dirty snow.

Just a girl? Jon obviously didn't have a clue.

Rosha wasn't "just" anything.

She was perfect.

Stopping for a red light, Brady slammed his fist against the steering wheel. He couldn't believe Jon. His best friend, calling him obsessed. A jerk. Letting him down.

The light changed to green. As Brady took off, he glanced in the rearview mirror.

A police car appeared behind him.

Had he been speeding?

Brady glanced nervously into the mirror again. The cruiser's turn signal went on and it made a left at the next block.

Brady breathed easier and told himself to calm down. He couldn't take any chances. Couldn't let his anger get him in trouble. He had to forget about Jon.

Forget about everything but finding Rosha.

The traffic lights were with him the rest of the way. Five minutes later Brady pulled to a stop across the street from St. Ann's.

The school was old, three stories high, built of dark red bricks. Steep stone steps led up to the front doors, which were closed.

Brady checked his watch. He'd made it with a couple of minutes to spare. He got out of the car and sat on the hood, his eyes on the front doors of the school.

He never heard a bell, but suddenly the doors burst open and a crowd of kids poured through them. They rushed down the steps in a blur of colorful winter jackets.

Brady climbed to his feet and tried to spot Rosha in the crush of students flowing out of the building.

There! Turning down the sidewalk, heading away from him! He couldn't see her face, but the hair was a match. Long and blond, spilling down her back in waves.

Brady jumped from the hood and tore across the street. "Rosha!" He edged his way through the crowd, leaped onto the sidewalk, and shouted her name again. "Rosha, wait! Rosha!"

The girl turned.

She wasn't Rosha. Not even close.

Brady stumbled to a stop, gaping stupidly at her.

She frowned at him and walked on.

Brady stared around. The crowd had thinned out now as kids reached their cars or caught buses.

He spotted three more blond-haired girls. None of them Rosha. *She could have left by the back doors,* he thought. *She might be on a bus or walking home, wherever that was.*

Brady pounded a fist against a car hood. What now? Go home and call more Nelsons? Hope Rosha called him?

He couldn't stand it.

He had to find her. Today!

Feeling desperate, Brady rushed up the front steps of St. Ann's and into the main hall. A few small groups of students lingered, chatting by their lockers. He could ask them about Rosha.

But he suddenly had a better idea. Brady hurried down the hall, checking the doors as he went. When he reached the principal's office, he took a deep breath and burst inside.

A stern-faced secretary glanced up from her computer. "Yes?"

"I have to find a friend of mine—a student here," Brady announced, trying to sound serious and concerned. "Her name is Rosha Nelson. Maybe you could tell me if she's still in the building. Or if she already left, I need her phone number."

The woman eyed him skeptically. "If she's a friend, surely you have her telephone number."

"Uh . . . yes, but I lost it," Brady told her quickly. "It's an emergency and I'm kind of upset. Could you just look her number up on the computer? It's really important."

"I'm sorry, young man. But I can't give out any information about our students," the woman informed him. "It's against school policy."

"But I'm her friend, and I'm telling you, it's an emergency!"

"Then I suggest you call the police. I really can't help you. I'm sorry." The woman swiveled back to her computer and began typing again.

Brady whirled around and left the office, gritting his teeth in frustration. As he pushed through the front door, he paused at the top of the steps and scanned the sidewalk, hoping to see Rosha.

But only one student remained near the school, standing next to a bus-stop bench.

A guy wearing a silver-and-blue St. Ann's jacket.

Brady smiled to himself.

A guy would have to be blind not to notice Rosha. This one might not know her. But Brady would bet anything he'd seen her.

And once any guy saw Rosha, he would remember her. Rosha was impossible to forget.

Brady trotted quickly down the steps and hurried to the bus stop. "Hey, I've got a problem," he told the guy waiting there. "I need to find a girl who goes here. Maybe you know her—Rosha Nelson?"

The guy immediately shook his head. "Never heard of her. I'd remember a weird name like that."

"Yeah, okay," Brady said. "But when I describe her, you'll know who I'm talking about. For sure." He quickly described Rosha. "Know who I mean now?"

The guy shook his head again.

"Oh, come on!" Brady protested. "There can't be another girl like that at St. Ann's."

"There's not even *one* girl like that at St. Ann's," the guy told him. "It's a small school. If your girl went here, I would have noticed her, believe me."

"But she told me she does!" Brady almost shouted.

"Yeah, well, she doesn't." The guy turned away and stared at the bus rolling toward them from down the street.

"I don't believe it!" Brady yelled. He grabbed the guy and spun him back around. "You're lying! Rosha goes to St. Ann's! Now tell me where she is!"

Brady knew he was losing it, but he couldn't stop himself.

"Tell me where she is!" he shouted. Without even realizing what he was doing, he shoved the boy backward. Watched as he went sprawling onto the sidewalk.

The boy's eyes grew wide. Frightened.

Brady clenched his fists.

What am I doing? he thought. *I'm losing it. I'm totally losing it.*

But this guy has *to know Rosha.*

And I'm going to make him tell me the truth.

11

"Are you *crazy*?" The boy scrambled to his feet, brushing dirty snow off his school jacket. His eyes were wide with shock. "What's your problem?"

Brady raised his fists, ready to punch the truth out of the guy. But the bus squealed to a stop next to them, spewing fumes.

The boy darted past Brady and jumped on board, glaring at Brady over his shoulder. The doors whooshed shut and the bus started down the street.

Brady stood alone on the corner, feeling stunned and angry.

Rosha said she went to St. Ann's. He could practically hear her saying the words!

Remembering the sound of Rosha's low, throaty voice, Brady groaned.

When would he hear it again?

Where was she?

I'm really losing it, he thought. *That poor kid thought I was nuts.*

Well, maybe I am.

Brady searched up and down the sidewalk. Deserted. He stuffed his hands in his jacket pockets and crossed the street toward the school. He hurried down a walkway that led to the back of the building.

St. Ann's football field was back there, he remembered.

And there it stood, covered in gray, slushy snow.

Brady started to leave.

But then he noticed a single figure standing deep in the shadows on the other side of the field.

A girl.

Her back was to Brady, so he couldn't see her face. She wore a knit cap on her head. A few strands of hair had escaped the cap and blew in the wind.

Brady couldn't tell whether it was blond.

But it was definitely long. As long as Rosha's.

Brady's heart raced with excitement. He took his hands from his pockets and began to jog across the field. As he drew closer, he saw that the girl's knit cap was purple.

Rosha's favorite color.

And her hair *was* blond.

It's Rosha! he thought, beginning to run full out. *It has to be!*

"Rosha!" he cried as he ran. "Hey, Rosha!"

The girl didn't turn.

"Rosha!" Brady shouted. Grinning in anticipation, he lunged the last few steps and grabbed hold of her arm.

As Brady spun the girl around, weak winter sunlight struck the girl's face.

Her hideously scarred face.

12

Brady dropped her arm and stumbled backward, his heartbeat drumming in his ears.

He had seen this girl before. On his date with Rosha. She'd stood in the shadows of the movie marquee.

Watching him.

Watching him with glittering eyes in a face totally covered with gnarled, twisted scars.

Brady felt disgust. Pity. Horror.

She doesn't even look human, he thought.

For a few seconds Brady stood rooted to the frosty grass on the football field, staring at the girl's face.

And then her eyes gleamed even more brightly from the folds of twisted flesh. She was going to speak to him!

No! Brady thought. He didn't know why, but

he couldn't stand the idea of listening to her. He spun quickly around, turning his back on the girl. As he hunched his shoulders and hurried away, he could feel her eyes on him.

Watching him again.

He broke into a run.

When he reached the other side of the field, he glanced over his shoulder.

The girl stood there, watching him.

Brady kept running, alongside the school building and across the street. As he sped along the sidewalk, he glanced back one more time.

And crashed into a figure stepping onto the sidewalk from behind his car.

A figure with green eyes and long blond hair swirling over the shoulders of her plum-colored jacket.

"Rosha!" Brady gasped.

"Brady, hi!" Rosha laughed and clung to his arm to keep from falling. "I can't believe it! What are you doing here?"

"I came to see you." Brady squeezed her hand and looked over his shoulder again. Had the scarred girl followed him?

"What are you looking at?" Rosha asked.

"A girl." Brady turned back to Rosha. "I saw her when we came out of the movie the other night.

And then I saw her a couple of minutes ago, standing by the football field. She gives me the creeps."

"Why?"

"Because of her face." Brady shuddered as he described the horrible scars.

Rosha shuddered, too, and stepped closer to him. "Let's drop it, okay?"

"Do you know her?" Brady asked. "I mean, she was standing in St. Ann's football field, so I figured you might have run into her in the hall."

Rosha shook her head. "I haven't. I don't know any girl with a scarred face."

"But . . ." Brady paused again.

Rosha tilted her head and gazed at him. "What's wrong?"

"It's just that I came here looking for you," Brady explained. "But the secretary wouldn't give me your number or anything. And then I ran into this guy outside. And he told me you didn't go here."

"So?" Rosha stared at him.

"It's weird, that's all," Brady told her. "I mean, I didn't believe him. I almost punched him out." He frowned. "But I don't get it. Why didn't he know you?"

"I don't believe this!" Rosha snapped. "You came here to check up on me?"

Brady stared at her, stunned by her anger.

"Why would I do something like that?"

"*You* tell *me*!" Rosha shouted. "I go to school at St. Ann's, okay? I'm new. I don't know many kids yet. So what if some guy you asked hasn't set eyes on me? How come you believe him instead of me?"

"I don't!" Brady cried. "I just said it was weird, that's all!"

"No! *You're* weird, Brady!" Rosha yelled. "Checking up on me. Asking a total stranger about me. You're much too weird!"

Before Brady could protest, Rosha spun around and stalked away.

13

Stunned, Brady stared after Rosha.

You jerk! he told himself. *What's the matter with you? She's getting away! Go after her and make it up to her!*

Brady's legs finally got the message from his brain. He tore across the street after Rosha and grabbed her arm.

"Rosha, I'm sorry!" he cried desperately. "Please. I didn't mean to make you angry. I wasn't checking up on you. I guess it sounded like that, but I really wasn't!"

Rosha didn't say anything. But she didn't pull away either.

"It's just that I wanted to see you so badly," Brady continued. "When I couldn't find you, I guess I went a little nuts. Then that girl with the scars surprised me, and I—" He broke off and took a deep breath. "I'm crazy about you, Rosha. Please don't be angry."

Rosha stared at him a moment longer.

Brady waited, his heart hammering. When Rosha's lips finally curved into a smile, he felt his knees wobble in relief.

She was going to forgive him!

Everything would be perfect again.

Rosha slipped her hand into his and leaned closer to him. Her silky hair brushed against Brady's cheek. It smelled like flowers. "You're crazy, all right," she murmured. "I think it must be that bump on your head. How is it, Brady? I've been worried out of my mind about you since the accident."

With Rosha standing so close, Brady barely remembered the lump on his forehead. "It's fine," he told her. "Really, Rosha. Nothing to worry about."

She squeezed his hand. "I feel really awful about the car, too," she told him. "I wish I could ask my dad to pay for the repairs. But I'm already in major trouble with him. If he finds out what happened, I'm afraid he'll ground me. And then I'd never see you again."

She really likes me, Brady thought happily. *She's been worried. She's been thinking about me.*

He could have floated into the sky.

"Don't worry about the car. The insurance took

care of it," he explained. "Hey, what are we doing standing around in the cold, anyway? Let's go get some coffee or a Coke or something."

"Sounds great," Rosha agreed. "But I only have half an hour. I have to get home and start a history paper."

Brady felt a stab of disappointment. Now that he'd finally found her, he wanted to spend hours with her. *Take what you can get,* he told himself.

In the car Brady spotted Rosha's black leather bag on the floor where he'd tossed it. "Oh, I've got something for you." He reached over, grabbed the bag, and handed it to her.

"My purse!" Rosha cried. "I've been wondering what happened to it!"

"You left it in the car after the movie," Brady explained, pulling the car away from the curb. "The police brought it over the next day."

"The police?" Rosha's eyes widened in alarm.

"No problem," he assured her. "I told them my girlfriend left it there on another date. They didn't have a clue you were with me that night."

Rosha sighed with relief. "Thanks, Brady."

"No problem," he repeated. "But it's weird. I mean, your bag is totally empty."

"You looked in my purse?" Rosha zipped open the bag and peered inside.

"Just to see if I could find your phone number," he told her quickly. He didn't want her to explode again. "But the bag was totally empty."

Spotting a coffee shop, Brady turned into the parking lot and found a space. He turned off the engine and glanced over at Rosha.

Rosha kept staring into the bag. "I remember now," she murmured. "I was so eager to meet you at the mall. It was all I could think about."

"You were eager to meet me?" Brady asked. That floating sensation returned, stronger than ever.

Rosha nodded, gazing at him shyly. "I must have spent an hour getting ready and then I ran out of the house with the wrong bag. Isn't that stupid?"

Brady gazed into her beautiful green eyes. "It's not stupid," he murmured. "It's great. Great that you wanted to see me, I mean. I couldn't wait to see you too."

Rosha's lips curved into a sexy smile. She tossed the bag aside and scooted across the car seat, settling next to Brady. She took his face in her hands and pulled it close to hers.

"I'm so glad we found each other again," she whispered, her lips brushing his. "I think we were meant to be together, don't you?"

"Definitely," Brady murmured.

Rosha's lips pressed against his. Soft at first,

then harder. Pulling back slightly, she kissed his cheeks, his forehead, his eyelids. Then she returned to his lips.

She's perfect, Brady thought, kissing her back. *Perfect.*

"You know what I want to do?" Rosha whispered, her breath tickling his ear.

"What?" Brady stroked her hair. "Anything."

"Go dancing Saturday night. Doesn't that sound great?"

"Saturday?" Brady frowned. Didn't he have something to do on Saturday?

"Yeah." Rosha's lips traveled from his ear to his cheekbone, then down to the corner of his mouth. "Don't you want to?"

"Definitely. Saturday night for sure," Brady agreed.

But even as he said it, Brady suddenly heard Allie's voice telling him about Mei Kamata's party.

Mei Kamata's ice-skating party.

On Saturday night.

Brady sighed.

"What's wrong?" Rosha murmured.

"Nothing," he assured her quickly. "Not a thing."

But as Rosha smiled and kissed him again, Brady's mind spun.

What am I going to do about Allie? he wondered.

Simple, Brady thought as he let himself in the front door of his house.

You're going to tell Allie the truth.

He tossed his jacket on the hall table and strode to the kitchen to find something to eat.

As he stared into the refrigerator, Brady imagined what he would say. *Listen, Allie, you're a terrific person and everything. But the thing is, I've met somebody else and I think we'd better break up.*

Short and sweet, right?

Brady shook his head.

Short. But not very sweet.

He grabbed a cold drumstick and a handful of napkins and took them upstairs to his room. Sitting on the bed, he gnawed the chicken and tried to figure out a better way to break it to Allie.

How else could he tell her? He couldn't go on and on about how perfect Rosha was. Not unless he wanted to hurt Allie and turn her into an enemy.

Which she probably would be anyway, no matter what he said.

Brady glanced guiltily at the phone.

Should he call Allie now and get it over with?

He shook his head again. *You're not ready yet,*

he told himself. *You'll wind up hurting her so badly she'll hate you forever.*

First he'd call Jon. He wanted to apologize for the way he'd acted after school. Plus, he wanted to tell Jon that he'd found Rosha.

Rosha. He grinned to himself.

Not only had he found her, but he'd found out she was crazy about him.

Her kisses proved it.

Still grinning, Brady finished the chicken and tossed it into the wastepaper basket.

As he wiped his fingers on the napkins, the phone rang.

Probably Allie, he thought, feeling guilty again. *Don't tell her yet. Wait until you come up with a good speech.*

He grabbed the phone. "Hello?"

"Hello, Brady." A girl's voice.

Brady shot to his feet, his heart hammering. It was the same voice. The same girl who'd called him before.

"Who is this?" he demanded. "What do you want?"

"I saw you," she replied. "I saw you with Rosha outside St. Ann's."

It's the girl with the scarred face! Brady realized. It has to be! Who else could have seen us there?

"Why have you been following me?" he demanded. "What do you want?"

"I already told you," the girl whispered. "Stay away from Rosha. This is no joke. Stay away from her."

"Forget it!" Brady shouted angrily. "Just leave me alone!"

Brady slammed the phone down and dropped onto the bed.

Who is she? he wondered, remembering the girl's hideously scarred face.

I don't know her.

Rosha doesn't know her.

What does she want with me? Why can't she just leave me alone?

"So you're going dancing with Rosha Saturday night?" Jon asked the next afternoon. He pulled open the door to the high school weight room. "What did Allie have to say about that?"

"Nothing. I didn't tell her about Rosha," Brady replied. "I just broke our date for Mei's party."

"What excuse did you give?"

"I told her I'm grounded because I haven't found a job to help pay for the car yet," Brady admitted.

Jon rolled his eyes and made his way over to a bench. Brady followed him.

The workout room was large and square, with mirrors on the walls, gray carpet on the floor, and state-of-the-art body-building machines. At the moment it was almost empty. But the smell of sweat lingered in the air.

Jon did a few warm-ups, then started in on some biceps curls with a set of weights. "And Allie bought it, huh?"

Brady nodded as he set up the bench-press machine next to Jon. "She was really steamed about the party," he said, lying back on the bench. "So it wasn't the right time to tell her about Rosha."

"Not the right time?" Jon's string-bean arms strained as he hefted the weights. "Are you for real? I say you're crazy for dumping her. But if you're going to do it, do it! You know what will happen if she finds out on her own—major trouble."

"I know, I have to tell her. I almost did. But at the last minute I just couldn't." Brady began lifting the weights, feeling the muscles in his arms swell. "I mean, at first she was really angry about Mei's party. Then she got all upset and almost cried."

"And you felt sorry for her," Jon declared.

"Yeah. I really like Allie," Brady told him, grunting as he pushed up the weights.

"But not as much as Rosha, right?"

Remembering the feel of Rosha's lips on his, Brady grinned. "What do you think?"

"I already told you what I think," Jon replied, puffing a little as he switched to heavier weights. "I think you've lost it. But hey, what do I know? Let's drop the subject before we get into another fight."

"Good idea." Brady smiled to himself again. So what if he'd lost it? Rosha was worth it. Too bad Jon didn't understand. But Brady felt better since they'd patched things up on the phone last night.

The phone.

Brady's satisfied smile faded.

In his mind, he heard the scarred girl's voice again.

Warning him.

Stay away from Rosha!

Brady shivered, even though the sweat was pouring off his face. His arms trembled. His breathing grew jerky.

"You okay?" Jon asked, wiping his forehead with the back of his wrist.

Brady rested the weights on his chest for a moment. "I don't know."

"What do you mean?" Jon asked him. "Is it your head?"

"No." Brady took a deep breath. "It's a girl."

"Huh? *Another* one?"

"Yeah, but it's not what you're thinking," Brady told him. "I don't even know who this one is. I mean, I've seen her. At least I think I have."

"Whoa." Jon raked his fingers back through his red hair. "I don't get it. Start at the beginning, okay?"

"Right." Slowly, Brady told him about the scarred girl. Watching him outside the movie theater.

And in the football field behind St. Ann's.

The girl with the ugly scars.

Watching him again.

And the two calls, warning him to stay away from Rosha.

"At first I didn't put it together," he explained. "The face and the calls, I mean. But when she called yesterday and said she'd seen me with Rosha, it clicked."

"Let me get this straight," Jon stated, frowning. "You think this girl with the scars is the same one warning you about Rosha."

Brady nodded.

"Weird," Jon commented. "Are you sure you don't know her?"

"Positive." Brady gripped the weights and shoved them above his chest. "And Rosha doesn't, either. But whoever she is, she really scares me."

Brady lowered the weights. *Forget about it,* he told himself. *Stop letting some strange girl creep you out like this*.

With a grunt he shoved the weights up. *Five more reps,* he decided. He lowered the weights, took a deep breath, and began to lift them again. Once. Twice.

He felt himself tiring. *Three more times,* he told himself. *Come on, just three more times.* He bit his lip, struggling to raise his arms to their full extension. Just a little bit higher. Higher.

A movement outside the window caught his eye. Brady blinked away a bead of sweat and turned his head on the padded bench.

A girl peered in at him.

The sunlight glanced off her scarred face.

The gleam from her slitted eyes seemed to burn through the glass.

Her scarred lips opened as if she were about to call his name.

No! Brady thought. He tried to shout, but his breath came in gasps.

Air. He couldn't get enough air. Couldn't breathe.

Fear pounded through Brady. His arms quivered violently.

The weights shook in his hands.

Brady gasped as his strength gave out.

The heavy, crushing weights dropped onto him like a high-speed elevator.

15

Pain shot through Brady's chest as the weights landed on him with a loud thud.

The air whooshed from his lungs. He scrabbled for a hold on the weights, tried to push them up again.

He couldn't breathe.

Couldn't move.

The weights were crushing him. Crushing out every bit of air.

Can't breathe. Going to die, Brady thought. *Suffocating.*

Jon's face appeared. Loomed over Brady. Jon's gray eyes wide with surprise.

Jon grunted loudly, and the pressing weight suddenly lifted from Brady's chest.

Brady opened his mouth and filled his lungs with air.

He rolled off the bench. Dropped to his knees. His chest throbbing with pain.

"What happened?" Jon cried. "Are you okay? What happened?"

"The girl!" Brady gasped hoarsely. "The scarred girl. At the window!"

Jon spun toward the window. He lurched over to it and peeked outside. Then he turned back to Brady, shaking his head. "Nobody out there."

"Not now, maybe!" Brady cried as he struggled to get up. "But she was. She was staring in, watching me!"

"Hey, come on!" Jon helped Brady sit on the bench. "Take it easy, okay? She's not there now. You sure you're not seeing things?"

"Seeing things?" Brady reached for his towel and wiped his face. "What are you talking about?"

"Well, you were just telling me about her." Jon shrugged and sat next to Brady. "She really creeps you out. She's on your mind, right? And then you think you see her."

"I *did* see her," Brady protested. He drew another gulp of air. His breathing began to slow. "But you're right about one thing—she creeps me out."

"Because of Sharon," Jon told him. "You're freaked because this scarred girl reminds you of Sharon."

Brady stared at him. "That's it," he murmured. "I can't believe I didn't get it before now. She *does* remind me of Sharon. Her face. All cut to pieces."

Brady breathed deeply and shut his eyes. Images flashed in his mind.

He was back on Miller Hill.

Staring at the gleaming white snow.

The steep hill, smooth as glass.

Feeling the cold air whistle past his ears.

Hearing Sharon Noles's voice scream in terror.

Watching her crash through the pines and the thornbushes.

Screaming all the way down to the bottom.

And then he saw her face when he turned her limp, dead body over.

The skin slashed to a pulp. Raw and mangled, bleeding into the snow. So cut up he couldn't recognize her.

Brady shuddered.

If Sharon hadn't died, her face would be scarred like that other girl's. That's why the sight of her frightened him so much. She reminded him of Sharon.

That explains my reaction, he thought. *But it doesn't explain the girl.*

Why has she been watching me?

Calling me?

Warning me about Rosha?

Brady's eyes snapped open. He stuffed the towel into his gym bag and jumped up from the bench.

Jon stared at him, a concerned expression on his face. "Where are you going?"

"To see Rosha," Brady told him. "I've got to talk to her about that girl."

"I thought Rosha didn't know anybody with a scarred face," Jon pointed out.

"I know. But there has to be some kind of connection between them. Maybe if I talk to Rosha, she'll remember something. There *has* to be a reason why this girl keeps warning me about her."

Jon frowned. "Listen, Brady. Be careful, okay?"

"What do you mean? I'm just going to talk to Rosha."

"I know, but this whole thing is weird." Jon wiped sweat off his forehead. "Don't beat up on me, man—but you have to admit, you don't know much about Rosha."

Brady shifted his weight impatiently. "I know all I need to know, Jon. She's perfect, okay? It's the *other* girl I'm worried about."

Jon started to say something, then shook his head. "Okay. Just take it easy. And good luck."

Hoisting his gym bag, Brady hurried out of the

weight room and pulled out his cell phone. He set his bag down and took out his wallet.

Carefully folded inside was a napkin with Rosha's address and phone number on it. She had written them down for him at the coffee shop yesterday, and he'd made sure to keep them in a safe place.

Brady punched in the numbers. One ring.

Two.

Then a shrill, electronic blast.

Brady winced and started to hang up.

Then a taped message came over the line. "The number you are calling is no longer in service."

I must have dialed it wrong, Brady thought. He tried again.

One ring. Two.

"The number you are calling is no longer in service," the recorded voice said again.

Brady ended the call angrily. What was going on?

He smoothed the napkin out and looked at his phone.

That's the number he called.

How could it be out of service? Rosha had written it herself. She couldn't possibly have gotten her own phone number wrong.

Weird.

Maybe the phone company had messed up somehow. Crossed signals or something. That must be it.

But he really needed to talk to Rosha. He had to find out if she knew that girl. He had to get to the bottom of this.

He glanced at the napkin again.

Rosha had written her address beneath the phone number.

7142 Fear Street.

Brady folded the napkin and put it back into his wallet. He picked up his bag and went into the boys' locker room.

A fast shower, some fresh clothes, and he'd be out of here.

On his way to Rosha's house.

I should have done this in the first place, he thought as he stood under the steaming spray of water. *Seeing Rosha face-to-face beats talking to her on the phone any day.*

Brady soaped and rinsed, toweled off quickly, and dressed in the jeans and maroon-and-gray Shadyside sweatshirt he had brought.

He ran a comb through his wet hair, grabbed his jacket, and hurried out to his car.

Brady drove through the business district on Division Street. He turned onto Mill Road and drove south until he came to Fear Street.

Fear Street was very different from North Hills, where Brady lived. His neighborhood was made up of large houses with neatly mowed lawns, carefully shoveled snow, no potholes in the streets.

The houses on Fear Street didn't follow any pattern. Some were mansions with peeling shingles and sagging gutters. Others looked clean and modern. Some old houses sprawled over huge yards. Others weren't much bigger than Brady's double garage.

Brady's heart pounded. Fear Street had a reputation for being strange. Sudden, unexplained drops in temperature. Kids disappearing. Weird howls in the woods at night.

But it's daytime, Brady reminded himself. *And I have to find Rosha.*

Brady sped through the first few blocks. Then he slowed the car, carefully checking the house numbers.

In the cemetery block he read the number 5657 on a tilted mailbox at the end of a driveway. Good. Rosha should be only a couple of blocks away.

He passed the cemetery and slowed to a crawl. *Talk about creepy!* he thought with a shudder. It looked so cold, with snow piled on the stone grave markers.

Sharon Noles was buried there. Brady had

watched her casket sink into the cold earth on a raw, gray day last winter.

They'd kept the casket closed at her wake.

Because of her face.

Her slashed, ruined face.

Brady never told anyone that Sharon didn't want to go down Miller Hill. Thinking about it now, he felt a sharp stab of guilt.

But it wasn't really his fault she died. Sure, she didn't want to sled there. But what happened was an accident.

Don't think about it, Brady commanded himself. *Don't think about Sharon.*

Find Rosha.

Across from the cemetery stood a house numbered 7023. It was on the left. So 7142 must be on the right. Brady slowed to a crawl again. Past one house. 7028.

Past a vacant lot.

Past more houses, one of them numbered 7030.

Brady inched along, counting houses in case Rosha's wasn't numbered. 7134. 7136.

And then—no more houses.

Brady braked, then backed up to the last house he'd passed.

He drove slowly forward again, glancing left and right.

He couldn't believe it. Nothing but woods stood on either side of the street.

No house numbered 7142.

No houses at all.

Nothing but woods as far as he could see.

16

The next afternoon Brady prowled the kitchen, opening cabinets and peering into the refrigerator without really seeing anything.

He felt fluttery. Totally stressed out.

All he could think about was Rosha.

Where was she?

Where could he find her? *How* could he find her?

He had tried her number a dozen times the day before—and heard the error message every time.

He called the phone company and talked to a human being who gave him the same message.

The number Rosha gave him was a nonworking number.

He had driven up and down Fear Street for twenty minutes, rechecking the house numbers. He stopped a kid on a bike and asked if he knew where the Nelsons lived.

The kid had never heard of the Nelsons.

And 7142 Fear Street didn't exist.

Brady slammed a cabinet shut and leaned against the counter.

No one knew Rosha Nelson at St. Ann's. No working phone number. No house on Fear Street.

It made no sense.

It was as if Rosha didn't exist!

But he had talked with her. Sat beside her in the movies. Held her hand.

Kissed her.

Brady shivered with pleasure, remembering Rosha's kisses. Rosha was out there somewhere, and he had to find her!

But he didn't have the first clue how to do it.

The kitchen clock caught Brady's eye. School had let out early today because of a teachers' conference. He had time on his hands, but the only thing he wanted to do with that time was spend it with Rosha.

Where was she? Why had she given him the wrong phone number? The wrong address?

Finally Brady gave himself a shake. If he stood around wondering about Rosha much longer, he'd go nuts.

Homework, he thought.

Brady grabbed a Mountain Dew out of the

refrigerator and carried his books into the living room. He spread the homework out on his dad's big wooden desk and reached for the bio notebook. As he flipped through the pages, he spotted Allie's handwriting. She'd copied her notes into his book a couple of weeks ago when he'd been out sick with a cold.

Allie.

Brady leaned back in the desk chair and thought about her. He knew she was still upset about the party. Maybe when he finished his homework, he would go see her. Not to tell her about Rosha—he wasn't ready to do that yet.

Without Rosha, he didn't have anything else to do.

After popping the tab on the soda can, Brady took a sip and flipped to the notes he needed to study.

Rosha's face drifted back into his mind. He tried to shake the image away, but the bio notes blurred. All he could see were Rosha's green eyes and pouty red lips.

Rosha's smile.

Her kisses.

He didn't want to study. He didn't want to go visit Allie. All he wanted was Rosha.

He couldn't get her out of his head.

The doorbell rang.

Brady jumped up and hurried out into the hall, hoping it would be Rosha. But even if it wasn't, he'd be glad for the distraction. He couldn't concentrate anyway.

The bell rang again. Brady eagerly pulled the door open and felt a wave of relief wash over him.

Rosha stood on the porch, looking beautiful in a purple skirt, a soft black sweater, and a black leather jacket.

Brady's heart beat faster at the sight of her. "Hey, this is perfect!" he exclaimed. "I was just thinking about you."

"I was thinking about you too, Brady." Rosha smiled—a sexy smile. "Fate, right?"

"Definitely," Brady agreed.

"I wasn't sure you'd be home. But I decided to take a chance and drop by." Rosha touched his arm. "I'm glad I did."

"So am I," Brady told her. "Really glad."

"Well?" She glanced over his shoulder. "Aren't you going to invite me in?"

"Oh—sure!" Brady stepped aside and let her into the front hall. "I'm really glad you came over," he repeated. "I wanted to see you, but I went looking for you yesterday and—"

"You did?" Rosha interrupted. "You're so sweet." She leaned close and kissed him.

Brady put his hands on her shoulders as he kissed her back.

"Let's sit down," Rosha suggested.

Brady took her hand and led her down the hall. As they entered the living room, Rosha tripped on the white throw rug that covered part of the polished wooden floor.

"Careful," Brady warned, tightening his grip on her hand to keep her from falling. "Everybody always trips over that rug."

"Maybe you should get rid of it," Rosha commented, steadying herself against the desk.

Brady laughed. "Try telling my mother that. Anyway, I went looking for you yesterday. But you gave me the wrong address or something."

Rosha raised her eyebrows. "I'm pretty sure I know where I live, Brady."

"Yeah, but check this out." Brady pulled out his wallet and removed the napkin. "See?" he asked, handing it to her. "Fear Street, right? Except there is no 7142 Fear Street. I drove there. No house. Just woods. What's the deal?"

"The deal is it's not 7142," Rosha replied, pointing to the napkin. "It's 1142. Can't you read?"

Brady snatched the napkin back and stared at the address. "It looks like a seven to me. But maybe the ink smeared."

"I'm sure that's what happened," Rosha agreed. She picked up a sword-shaped silver letter opener from the desk and ran her thumb along the blade. "1142 is the big gray house on the corner. I guess you drove right past it. What a shame."

"Yeah. Except . . ." Brady paused.

Sighing impatiently, Rosha slapped the blade of the letter opener against her palm. "Except what?"

Brady glanced at her. "Your phone number?"

"What about it?"

"Before I tried to find your house, I called you," Brady told her. "But I kept getting a recording that said it was a nonworking number. I called the phone company, too, and they told me the same thing."

Rosha shrugged. "Well, don't ask me. I mean, the phone was working fine this morning."

"It was?"

"Of course it was!" she exclaimed. "What is this—a court trial?"

Brady shook his head. "Of course not—"

"Brady, what's your problem?" Rosha demanded. "You read my house number wrong. And you know the phone company—they're always messing up. Why are you checking on me again? Why are you always so suspicious?"

Brady frowned, confused. "It's just that . . ."

A car door slammed outside.

Brady made his way to the front window and pulled back the curtain.

Allie's car sat in the driveway. Allie's auburn hair glinted red in the afternoon sun as she hurried up the walk toward the front door.

Brady dropped the curtain and spun around. "It's Allie!" he cried, panic in his voice.

"Who?" Rosha asked.

"Never mind!" Brady glanced around, feeling trapped. "Listen, Rosha, I can't explain right now. But you've got to leave."

"Leave?"

"Yeah. And I know it sounds crazy, but could you go out the back way?"

Brady jumped as the doorbell rang. "Hurry!" he pleaded. "I'll explain everything later!"

"Okay, I guess." Rosha gave him a confused smile and started across the room toward the door.

The doorbell rang again.

"Thanks, Rosha," Brady told her gratefully. "Listen, I'll call you later and we can . . . look out!" he cried as the toe of Rosha's boot caught on the edge of the throw rug.

Rosha gasped and started to fall. Her arms flailed the air as she tried to catch her balance.

Brady grabbed her arm, trying to keep her from falling.

Rosha swung her other arm to clutch his shoulder.

Instead, she hit his side.

Brady felt something cold against his skin.

Then he felt a burning sensation.

Pain.

His side was on fire. He screamed. Grabbed at his waist.

The pain blazed through him. He yanked his hand away.

The furniture began to spin. Dizzy, Brady gazed down at himself.

Something silver poked out through his shirt.

With a strangled cry, Brady realized what it was.

The handle of the letter opener.

But he could see only part of the blade.

Because the rest of it was buried in Brady's skin.

17

Brady gasped. The room spun. Blackness edged his vision.

The pain grew sharper as it spread over his body. He uttered a low moan.

Rosha cried out in horror. "Oh no! Oh, Brady, what have I done?"

Brady screamed again as Rosha grabbed the letter opener with both hands—and yanked it out. His vision began to blur and his legs wobbled. He fell to the floor.

Rosha's voice seemed to come from very far away. "I'm so sorry!" she exclaimed frantically. "Oh, Brady, are you okay?"

Dark red blood seeped from Brady's wound. Formed a widening circle on his pale blue shirt. He felt the thick, sticky wetness oozing through his fingers. Saw it trickle onto the white rug beneath him.

He moaned again, tightly clutching his side.

Rosha knelt beside him, her hand gently on his arm, her green eyes wide with fear. "You'll be okay, I'm sure you'll be okay!" she cried. "I'll get you to a hospital, Brady, don't worry!"

Brady gritted his teeth as the fierce pain bit into him. Beads of sweat popped out on his face. His body trembled. Every breath was agony.

"Yeah," he muttered, his jaw clenched. "The . . . hospital." He took a shallow breath. Tried not to scream again.

The front door slammed. "Brady?" Allie's worried voice called out. "Brady!"

Footsteps pounded down the hall toward the living room. "Brady, what's wrong?" Allie cried. "I heard you scream— "

Brady heard Allie's sudden gasp. The rug muffled her footsteps as she quickly approached him.

Another sharp gasp.

"Oh no!" Allie shrieked. "Brady! Brady, what happened? What happened? What did she do to you?"

"She . . . she . . ." Brady peered up at Allie through the blackness that threatened to engulf him. He tried to say more, but he couldn't get enough breath.

Rosha jumped up, still gripping the letter opener.

"What happened? Who are you?" Allie asked Rosha. Her gray eyes widened in horror as she saw the blood dripping from the silver blade onto the white rug. "You stabbed him! You stabbed Brady!"

"It was an accident!" Rosha cried. She flung the letter opener aside and dropped to her knees next to Brady. "I tripped on the rug. I forgot I had the letter opener in my hand. It was an accident. I'd never hurt him on purpose!"

"Who *are* you?" Allie demanded again.

"What difference does it make?" Rosha shouted. "Help me. Help me or he'll bleed to death! We've got to get him to the hospital!"

Rosha gently slipped her hand under Brady's arm. Allie took hold of the other one.

As the two girls tried to lift him to his feet, searing pain sliced through Brady's side again.

Pinpoints of light danced in front of his eyes.

His vision grew dim.

The blackness closed in.

Something cool touched Brady's forehead. Something gently stroked his hair back.

Fingers, Brady thought. Cool fingers. Felt so good.

As he began to open his eyes, a wave of nausea washed over him. He closed them.

"Brady?" a voice murmured.

Brady licked his lips. "Mom."

His mother brushed his hair back again. "Your dad and I are both here, honey. You're in Shadyside Hospital."

"You're going to be fine, son," his father's gruff voice assured him. "You'll be out shoveling the front walk in no time."

Brady started to laugh. The pain slammed into his side.

The laugh turned into a groan. Sweat bathed his forehead. "No joking yet," he gasped.

"Sorry," his father murmured, patting his shoulder.

"Brady, honey, you should sleep some more," his mother told him. "The doctor said we could only stay a few minutes. If he finds us here when he comes back, he'll kick us out."

"We'll go down to the cafeteria and have some coffee," Brady's father said. "You sleep. We'll be back in a little while."

Brady felt his mother kiss his forehead. Heard the two of them tiptoe out of the room. He tried opening his eyes again, but he couldn't focus.

Pain hammered at his side.

But he'd be all right.

He lay quietly, taking small, shallow breaths—

and remembered what had happened.

Allie coming to the door.

Rosha tripping on the rug.

Then the pain.

The blood.

Rosha horrified. Allie screaming. Both of them trying to help him up.

More searing pain. Then nothing.

Until now.

Brady gritted his teeth. His side felt tight. Stitches, probably. It still throbbed and burned.

Hadn't the doctor given him anything for the pain? He must have. That's probably why he felt so groggy. But he could use another shot or pill or something.

Brady was trying to get up the strength to move, to look for a call button, when he heard the door whoosh open.

Footsteps approached the bed.

A nurse, he thought. *Good. Time for some medicine. And some water.* His mouth felt full of dust.

He opened his eyes.

Nausea hit him again, but not as bad.

A pale blob hovered above him. Blurred and fuzzy. A face, he figured.

"I want some water," he murmured. "And my side hurts. It's pretty bad."

The blob nodded. Brady blinked, trying to bring the face into focus.

Why wasn't the nurse moving?

"So," he mumbled groggily. "Can you help me?"

"That's what I'm here for, Brady," a voice replied.

"Good. I . . ." Brady stopped.

He'd heard that voice before. Twice before.

On the telephone.

Warning him to stay away from Rosha.

Panic flooded him, but he couldn't run. He couldn't move.

Gradually his vision cleared.

The scarred girl stared down at him.

Her eyes glittered angrily from their swollen sockets. Her lips twisted back. The scars crawled across her face like worms.

Brady gasped. Why was she here? Who let her in? "Don't worry, Brady," she told him. "I didn't come here to hurt you."

Brady's heart pounded. The pulse throbbed in his wound. He sucked in a hissing breath. "Wh-what do you want?" he stammered.

"To see if you're ready to listen to me now," the girl replied. "You didn't before. I warned you. I warned you, but you didn't listen. And look what happened to you."

Brady rolled his head on the pillow. "Accident," he muttered.

"It was no accident!" the girl insisted.

"Who are you?" Brady asked. "Why are you doing this?"

"I'm not doing it. Don't you understand?" she snapped. "It's Rosha! *She's* doing it! Rosha wants to kill you, Brady! And she almost did!"

"Kill me?" Brady whispered.

"Yes!" the girl hissed. "She already tried twice. Do you want to know the truth about Rosha? Do you want to listen now?"

Brady licked his lips again. Thought of Rosha. The perfect girl. He nodded. "Tell me."

The girl leaned over his bed.

Brought her scars closer.

Her ugly face only a foot from Brady's.

"Rosha is . . ."

18

The door whooshed open. The girl jumped back.

Footsteps rapidly approached the bed. A doctor peered at Brady, then frowned at the girl. "No visitors, miss," he ordered sternly. "This patient needs his rest. How did you get in here?"

The girl remained silent.

"Well, you shouldn't be here," the doctor told her. He grabbed her arm and began pulling her away from the bed.

"Wait!" Brady cried.

"Are you in pain?" the doctor asked him, still pulling the girl toward the door. "I'll send a nurse. Come on," he added to the girl.

"Wait!" Brady cried again, struggling to sit up. "Wait! Don't go!"

Too late. The door closed. The girl was gone.

Brady sank back against the pillow, gasping with pain. And with fear.

What did the scarred girl know about Rosha? What had she started to tell him?

On Saturday morning Brady gingerly eased himself into the back seat of his family's car.

"Careful, Brady," his mother warned anxiously, standing beside him. "Just get yourself in and I'll buckle the seat belt for you."

"Thanks, Mom, but give it a rest, okay?" Brady's side was still sore, but he felt much stronger. "I'm not an invalid."

"Of course not. But you *are* weak," his mother replied.

"You lost a lot of blood," his father added.

"Yeah, but I'm not too weak to fasten my own seat belt." Brady pulled the belt over and snapped it in place. "See? I didn't even break a sweat."

His mother laughed. "All right, all right. We'll stop hovering. But you do have to take it easy for a while."

As his father pulled the car out of the hospital parking lot, Brady leaned back in the seat and gazed out the window, thinking.

Physically, he could take it easy. No problem.

But his mind was another story. It wouldn't

keep still. Hadn't kept still ever since he'd seen that girl in his hospital room. Standing by his bed. Glaring down at him and warning him again.

Rosha wants to kill you, she'd said.

Unbelievable.

Rosha is bad news, Jon told him when he came to visit at the hospital. *She's been nothing but trouble for you since the day you met her.*

True, Brady had to admit. Rosha had scalded his hand, wrecked his dad's car, stabbed him. Definitely accidents. But major trouble, especially the last one.

But it didn't make any difference.

He couldn't stop thinking of her.

He couldn't wait to see her again.

Rosha hadn't visited him in the hospital. Too ashamed, Brady figured. Feeling too guilty to face him.

But he'd find her soon. Hold her and kiss her. Tell her it wasn't her fault.

And everything would be perfect.

"Looks as if you have a visitor," Brady's dad remarked as he turned the car into the driveway.

Brady leaned forward and gazed through the windshield.

A girl stood on the front porch. A yellow cap covered her hair. The ends of a purple muffler hung down her back.

Purple. *Could it be Rosha?* Brady wondered. His heart started pounding in anticipation.

The girl turned at the sound of the car.

Strands of auburn hair peeked out from the front of the hat. Disappointed, Brady slumped back against the seat.

Not Rosha.

Allie.

Allie had come to the hospital. He'd been groggy from the painkillers, so she didn't stay long. But she came to see him. She sent him flowers and a funny card, too.

But Rosha is the one I want, Brady thought. *I can't help it. I can't help it!*

Allie waved and waited for the Karlins to join her on the porch. "I hope you don't mind having a visitor so soon," she told Brady.

"Are you kidding?" Brady smiled, hiding his disappointment. "If you weren't here, Mom would make me get into bed. And she'd take my temperature every half hour." They all entered the house. "Let's go into the den and you can catch me up on everything I've missed," he told Allie.

Brady's parents went upstairs. Allie followed Brady into the den across the hall from the kitchen.

"Hey, thanks for the card and the flowers," Brady told her. He shrugged off his jacket and sank into the leather recliner. "They were great."

"You're welcome." Allie stood in front of the fireplace and stared into it, even though no fire was burning. "How are you feeling, Brady?"

"Not bad." Brady swung his feet onto the ottoman. "Just a little sore and kind of tired. But the doctor says I'll be back in shape real fast."

"That's good." Allie continued to stare into the empty grate.

"Why don't you sit down?" Brady suggested. "Take off your coat. Want something to drink?"

"Thanks, but I'm not staying long." Allie turned around. Her gray eyes narrowed as she stared at him. "That should make you happy, right?"

"What do you mean?" he asked.

"I mean, you probably can't wait until I leave so you can call your new girlfriend," she explained.

Brady felt his face heat up. "Listen, Allie— "

"No." Allie held up her hand to cut off his words. "You listen, Brady," she told him. "When I came into your house the other day and saw you lying there . . . bleeding . . . I thought that girl had stabbed you. I mean, I thought she was some psycho stranger who broke into your house or something."

Brady kept quiet.

"But then on the way to the hospital, she set me straight," Allie continued. She shook her head. "Boy, did she set me straight!"

"Allie, I—"

"How could you do that to me, Brady?" Allie demanded. "How could you pretend we were going together when you were seeing somebody else at the same time?"

Brady shook his head. "I don't know," he admitted. "I just couldn't figure out a way to tell you, I guess."

"So you lied to me." Allie gazed at him, a sad, disappointed expression in her eyes. "You should have been honest, Brady. You shouldn't have been sneaking around with another girl."

"Yeah," Brady agreed. "I'm sorry, Allie. You're right. I'm really sorry."

"So am I."

Brady stood up. "Well. Now that you know the truth, I guess you don't want to go out with me anymore, huh?"

"I guess not." Allie gazed at him a moment longer, then crossed to the door. "Good-bye, Brady."

Brady waited until he heard the front door close. Then he sighed and went into the kitchen. He grabbed a bag of pretzels from the cabinet and started up the stairs to his room.

His mother met him on her way down. "Did Allie leave already?" she asked.

"Uh, yeah. She couldn't stay long," Brady told her.

"Well, you need to rest, anyway. Your father went to the office to catch up on some work, and I'm going out to the store." She patted him on the shoulder. "You'll be all right, won't you?"

"Stop worrying, Mom. I'm fine."

I actually am *fine,* Brady thought as he climbed the stairs.

Sure, he felt bad about Allie.

But he felt relieved, too.

No more lying or sneaking around. From now on, he and Rosha could see each other any time. Any place.

In his room Brady broke open the bag and ate a handful of pretzels. They tasted great, especially after the cardboard stuff they served him at the hospital.

He kicked off his shoes and carefully stretched out on the bed. As he reached for the telephone to call Rosha, it rang. "Hello?" he answered.

"Brady." Jon's voice sounded relieved. "Good, you're okay."

"I'm great! Stop acting like my mother." Brady stuffed another pretzel into his mouth. "What's up?" he mumbled.

"Plenty. Can you come over?" Jon asked. "We have to talk!"

"About what?" Brady heard the tension in his friend's voice. "What's wrong, Jon? You sound really stressed."

"I am. I found out some stuff about Rosha," Jon replied. "You won't believe it."

"What?" Brady sat up quickly, wincing as the stitches in his side pulled. "What did you find out?"

"It's that girl!" Jon exclaimed. "The one with the scars. She—"

"Wait a minute," Brady broke in. "I thought we were talking about Rosha."

"We are. Just listen. That girl with the scars is here." Jon lowered his voice. "Major weirdness, man. But I think it's true. The girl says—"

A beep sounded in Brady's ear. "Hold on a sec, Jon. It's my call-waiting. Let me see who it is."

Hoping to hear Rosha's husky voice, Brady pushed the button to take the call on the other line. "Hello? Hello?"

No one answered.

Brady pushed the button again. "I'm back, Jon."

Silence.

"Jon? You there?"

No answer.

Brady hung up, then punched in Jon's number.

The phone rang five times. Ten. Fifteen.

Brady hung up. *Jon has to be home,* he thought. *I was talking to him ten seconds ago. His phone must be messed up or something.*

He tapped the telephone nervously. Picked it up and dialed Jon again.

Still no answer.

What had Jon learned about Rosha? He sounded really upset.

And why didn't he answer the phone?

Brady pulled his shoes back on and hurried downstairs. He slipped his car keys off the hook in the kitchen, grabbed his jacket from the den, and hurried outside.

A light snow had started to fall. Brady shrugged into his jacket and strode quickly to his car. His side ached a little. His mother was going to kill him for going out—but he'd worry about that later.

He had to find out what Jon knew.

Jon lived six blocks away, in the last house on a dead-end street. The snow began falling a little harder as Brady drove. Fat, icy flakes built up on the windshield. The wipers worked, but the defroster groaned once and then conked out.

Rosha, Brady thought. *I'll find out about Rosha. And about that girl with the scars.*

By the time Brady pulled onto Jon's street, the

car windows had totally fogged up on the inside. He steered with one hand and used his other arm to wipe the mist from the glass.

Swirling red and blue lights appeared through the sheet of falling snow. *That's weird,* Brady thought.

He hitched forward in the seat and peered through the smeared windshield.

"Huh?" Police cars?

Yes.

Two police cars stood in Jon's driveway.

A third stood half-on, half-off the curb, its rear end jutting into the street.

The front door to Jon's house stood wide open.

Brady hit the brakes. The car skidded to a stop, barely missing the third patrol car. He flung open the door and jumped out. His heart hammered as he raced across the snow-crusted yard, up the slippery stone steps, and into Jon's house.

A police officer stood inside the front door.

"What's happening?" Brady cried. "What's going on?"

"Are you a member of the family?" the policeman asked, not answering Brady's question.

"No, I'm a friend. What's going on? Where's Jon?" Brady heard voices and movement in the living room. "Jon?" he called, starting down the hall.

"Hey, you can't go in there!" The officer reached out to stop him. But Brady shook his hand off and ran the few steps to the arched door of the living room.

The room was crowded with cops, muttering in grim, low tones. Brady pushed through them, scanning the room, searching for Jon.

And then he saw him.

Jon lay sprawled between the couch and the coffee table. Arms flung above his head. Mouth open in a frozen scream. Red hair fluttering in the cold breeze from the open front door.

Brady's pulse thundered in his ears as he stared down at what remained of his best friend. "Wh-what—?" he choked out.

"His neck is broken," Brady heard a policeman mutter.

"Windpipe crushed," another officer said, shaking his head.

Brady stared in shocked horror.

Jon's eyes stared at the ceiling. Past the police officers. Past Brady.

His throat! Brady thought, the panic rising.

A heavy marble candlestick lay across Jon's neck.

Pressed into the soft flesh.

Crushing Jon's throat.

19

A heavy hand landed on Brady's shoulder.

He turned from Jon's crushed body and stared up at a middle-aged policeman with piercing dark eyes.

"You know this kid?" the officer asked.

Brady nodded. "He's . . ." He swallowed hard. "He was my best friend. Jon Davis. I was talking to him. Just a few minutes ago."

"Oh?" The officer's hand tightened on Brady's shoulder. "And where did this conversation take place?"

"Not here," Brady told him quickly. "On the phone. He called me at home. He was worried because . . ." His gaze drifted back to Jon. He began to shake.

"Let's go in another room," the cop suggested. "I have to ask you some questions. Come on."

Feeling like a sleepwalker, Brady let the officer guide him out of the living room and down the hall to the kitchen. A policewoman joined them.

Brady sat down shakily at the round wooden table. He and Jon used to pig out on junk food at this table. Play cards. Talk about cars and girls.

Girls.

Rosha.

What did Jon find out about her?

"Okay." The dark-eyed officer interrupted Brady's thoughts. "Tell us your name, son. Name, address, phone number."

The policewoman pulled a pen from her pocket and flipped open a small spiral notebook.

Brady gave the information. He gazed at the refrigerator. A yellow banana-magnet clamped Jon's senior picture to its door. Jon gazed out, freckle-faced and smiling.

Brady drew in a shuddering breath and lowered his eyes.

"All right, Brady. Jon called you. He was worried."The dark-eyed officer hitched his chair closer to the table. "What was he worried about?"

"I don't know for sure," Brady replied. "My call-waiting beeped. Must have been the wrong number, though, because nobody answered.

Anyway, when I came back to Jon, he wasn't on the line anymore."

That's when someone attacked him, Brady thought. *That's when Jon died.* He shuddered again.

"We know what a shock this is, Brady," the second officer said softly. "A neighbor walked through the open door and found Jon. We're through questioning him. Someone is notifying Jon's parents right now. They'll be here soon. So help us out. We know it's hard. But you have to tell us whatever you know."

"Sure." Brady's hands shook. He clasped them on the table. "Okay. When Jon called, he said somebody was here."

The officer leaned forward. "Who? Did he say who?"

Brady nodded. "A girl. A girl with scars all over her face."

As the second police officer scribbled in her notebook, Brady described the scarred girl.

Then he told them everything he knew.

How the girl had been watching him. Calling him.

Warning him about Rosha.

How she showed up in his hospital room. Told him Rosha wanted to kill him.

"When Jon called, he said the scarred girl was here," Brady repeated. "He told me he learned something about Rosha. But he never got the chance to tell me what. And I don't know who the scarred girl is. I don't know anything about her!"

"We'll find her," the first officer assured him. He motioned to his partner, who left the kitchen.

"Do you think she killed Jon?" Brady asked.

The policeman shook his head. "No idea yet. We'll know more when we find her and ask her some questions." He shoved his chair back and stood up. "I think that's enough now, Brady. I'll get one of my officers to drive you home."

"No, that's okay." Brady got to his feet. "I have my car."

Besides, he wanted to be alone.

The officer escorted him out of the kitchen and down the hall. As they passed the living room, Brady glanced quickly inside.

Jon's broken body still lay sprawled in front of the couch.

Brady stumbled, caught himself, then hurried out the front door.

Snow continued to swirl down, heavier now. Brady's earlier footprints were almost filled.

He used his bare hands to shove the snow

from the windshield, then climbed into his car and started home.

Snow covered the road. The car skidded as Brady turned the corner, almost spinning around. Brady twisted the wheel. The tires spun.

Slow down, Brady told himself. *Concentrate on the road.*

But the image of Jon's flattened body kept flashing through his mind.

And questions kept swirling in his head.

Did the scarred girl kill Jon?

Why?

Who is she?

What did Jon learn about Rosha? Something the scarred girl didn't want him to know? It didn't make sense.

Nothing made sense.

The car skidded again. Headlights flashed in Brady's eyes. A horn honked angrily. Brady clamped his hands on the wheel and gritted his teeth as he steered around the oncoming car.

Just get home, he thought. *Get home and call Rosha. She has to know that girl! She has to have some answers!*

After a few more skids, Brady finally reached his house. No car tracks in the driveway. His parents weren't back yet.

Brady trudged up the snowy walk and onto the porch. He stamped his feet on the mat and shoved open the door.

In the silence of the house he heard the answering machine click off.

It was Mom, Brady thought, tracking snow into the living room. *She's stuck at the store. Wants me to come get her.*

He walked to the desk and punched the button to hear the message.

"Hi, Brady!" Rosha's voice sounded happy. Excited. "Just wanted to make sure we're still on for dancing later tonight—if your injury is better! Plus, if you get home in time, why don't you come to the park? I'm going there right now to go sledding. Please come if you can. Bye, Brady!"

The answering machine clicked off.

"I'm on my way, Rosha," Brady murmured. "I'm definitely on my way!"

He hurried out of the living room and down the hall. Snow blew into his face as he yanked open the front door. Brady tugged it shut behind him and sprinted down the steps to his car.

The wheels spun as he sped out of the drive.

I have a lot of questions, Rosha, Brady thought as the car rocked and slithered its way down the snow-covered road toward Shadyside Park.

Like why did the scarred girl kill Jon?

And what do you know about her, Rosha? You have to know something.

And for once I'm going to get some answers!

20

Wind-driven flakes pelted the side of Brady's car and blew into his face through the car window. He had to keep it open so the windshield wouldn't fog up.

Ignoring the icy sting on his skin, Brady hunched over the steering wheel and squinted into the blurry whiteness.

Shadyside High appeared. Snowdrifts curled like waves against its walls.

It had taken fifteen minutes to get this far. It should have taken about three.

Brady cautiously made the turn onto Park Drive. The rear end of the car swung wide. He twisted the wheel. The car slithered sideways. The tires spun, then finally dug in.

Brady let his breath out and gently pressed the gas pedal.

He had to see Rosha. He had to get some answers!

But the roads were treacherous.

Brady had to keep the car at a crawl. He clenched his jaws and cursed the weather.

Past the school now. Not much farther to the park.

The car inched forward through the piling snow.

A hill rose ahead. Not a steep one, but in this weather any hill was a problem.

Brady floored the gas pedal, hoping to get a running start.

The tires spun and whined. No traction at all. The car shuddered, then began to backslide.

As the car coasted backward, Brady turned the wheel and let it drift toward the curb.

The park is only a block away, he thought. *Close enough.* He shoved the door open and stepped into the whirling snow.

Get to Rosha and get some answers!

The cold pierced his jacket as he plunged through a snowdrift and into the park. Without gloves, his hands felt like blocks of ice. The stitches in his side pulled painfully.

But Rosha said she'd be here. He had to talk to her!

By the time Brady reached the bottom of Miller Hill, the cold had seeped deep inside him, chilling his bones.

Shivering violently, he gazed up the steepest sledding hill in the park.

Impossible to see anything but blowing snow.

He sucked in a deep breath of icy air. "Rosha!" he shouted. "Rosha!"

The wind snatched the sound and spun it away.

He cupped his hands around his mouth and screamed again. "Rosha! Rosha!"

No answer. Just the tick, tick of icy snowflakes blowing against his jacket.

Had Rosha changed her mind and returned home once she saw how bad the storm was?

You've come this far, Brady thought to himself. *Go on up. Check out the top of the hill first, just to make sure.*

He paused a moment and tried to still his shaking muscles. Tried to gather some strength. Usually he'd approach Miller Hill from the other side, a gentle slope. No chance of that now.

Go on, he told himself. *Climb it. Rosha might be up there.*

Thinking of Rosha gave him some energy. Brady drew more freezing air into his lungs and began the steep climb.

His legs sank deep into snow with each step. Halfway up the steep hill, he leaned against a pine tree to rest. He caught his breath, then tried calling Rosha again.

Still no response.

But she might be up there, Brady. She might be waiting for you. Don't turn back now!

He plunged ahead.

Using bushes and tree trunks to help pull himself up, Brady finally staggered onto the top of Miller Hill.

He bent over, gasping for a moment. The wound in his side throbbed. He straightened up slowly and glanced around.

The snow had let up. The clouds had begun to thin. *Storm is almost over,* he thought.

But no sign of Rosha.

Had she left already? Was he too late?

"Rosha!" he shouted. "Rosha, are you up here?"

He trudged over and peered down the short side of the hill.

No one in sight.

Brady shoved his cold hands deep into his jacket pockets and glanced around again.

There!

Running toward him along the ridge. Honey-blond hair flying out behind her. Legs pumping through the snow. Red lips open in a smile.

"Brady!" Rosha called out.

He raised his arm and waved.

A surge of warmth pumped through him as he hurried to meet her. Warmth and relief. Now they could talk.

They met at the center of the hilltop. Rosha threw her arms around Brady's neck. "I'm so glad you came, Brady!" she cried, clinging tightly to him.

Brady held her close. "I'm glad you're here," he murmured into her silky hair. "I was afraid you left."

"Of course I didn't leave." Rosha kissed his cheek. Tilted her head back and smiled at him. "I've been waiting for you, as I said I would."

Brady gazed into her sparkling green eyes. "Rosha—"

"Isn't it great out here?" Rosha interrupted, glancing around the snow-covered hill. "Aren't you glad you came?"

Brady ignored the view. "Yeah. But, Rosha, I have to talk to you."

"Sure, Brady—talk!" She laughed and kissed his cheek again. "Ooh, your face is so cold!"

"Yeah. The snow really did a number on me," Brady admitted.

"You poor thing!" Rosha slipped her arm

around his waist. "I'm so sorry I made you come out in this storm. But look," she added, pointing toward the sky. "It's over now."

As Brady looked up, sunlight broke through the clouds. It shone on Rosha's blond hair and sparkled on the snowy slope of Miller Hill.

"It's beautiful, isn't it?" Rosha repeated, gazing down the steep hill. "Perfect, don't you think?"

But Brady wasn't interested in the view. He had to tell Rosha about Jon and the scarred girl. He had to get some answers to his questions.

"Rosha— "

She turned to him, cutting off his words again. "Looks just the way it did on our sledding afternoon, doesn't it?" she asked.

"Huh?" Brady frowned. "What are you talking about?"

"Our sledding afternoon," Rosha repeated.

Brady stared at her, totally confused. "We never— "

"Don't tell me you've forgotten, Brady," Rosha interrupted. "*I* haven't forgotten. After all, that was the day you killed me."

21

Brady gaped at her, baffled. "What are you talking about?"

Rosha's grip tightened around Brady's waist. Her sexy, throaty voice turned harsh. "Can't you figure it out? I'm not Rosha. I'm Sharon."

"You're crazy!" Brady cried. "Sharon is dead!"

"Not anymore." Rosha's beautiful mouth curved into a smile.

A dangerous smile.

Brady tried to step away, but Rosha's arm tightened around his waist.

Held him. Trapped him.

"You're crazy!" Brady repeated. "You can't be Sharon!"

"Can't you figure it out, Brady?" Rosha demanded coldly. "I'll give you a clue."

"Rosha, what—"

"The clue is in my name," she told him. "Rosha Nelson? Sharon Noles? Ever hear of anagrams, Brady?"

"What?" Brady's mind whirled. "Anagrams? But, Rosha. You can't— "

"You don't get it!" Rosha tossed her hair and laughed sarcastically. "You're totally stumped! Unbelievable! I don't know what I ever saw in you."

"Rosha . . . ," Brady started again.

"I'm Sharon!" Rosha insisted. Her green eyes glittered angrily. "Think about it, Brady. An anagram is when you jumble the letters of a word and make another word out of them."

Even in shock, Brady's mind jumbled the letters of Sharon Noles and turned them into Rosha Nelson.

Rosha Nelson. Sharon Noles.

"Very good, Brady," Rosha declared. "I see you get it now. How come you didn't get it sooner? Couldn't you recognize the girl you killed?"

"You're nuts!" Brady yelled. He wrenched himself free from her grip and stumbled back. "You're totally crazy! Sharon is dead! She fell and died. I didn't kill her!"

Rosha's hand shot out and grabbed his arm. "Look, Brady!" she ordered, pointing down the steep slope. "Look at Miller Hill! Remember that afternoon, a year ago?"

Brady gazed down the steep hill.

"I didn't want to sled on it, remember?" Rosha muttered. "I thought it was too dangerous. I was afraid. But you forced me."

"No!"

"Shut up and listen, Brady!" Rosha hissed in his ear. "I told you I didn't want to sled down it, but you made me. You grabbed me and pushed me onto my sled. I kept saying I didn't want to do it, remember? But you didn't listen! You shoved my sled over the edge of the hill. You forced me. And you killed me!"

"You're crazy!" Brady screamed. "You're crazy!"

"Of course I'm crazy!" Rosha laughed wildly.

Brady tried to pull away again. Her fingers dug painfully into his arm. Kept him close to her.

"Of course I'm crazy," Rosha repeated. "That's why I came back—back from the dead—to kill you!"

"But you're *not* Sharon!" Brady protested, staring at Rosha's beautiful face. "You don't look anything like Sharon! She had light brown hair. Blue eyes. She—"

"Oh, Brady, you're really so stupid!" Rosha exclaimed in disgust. "My plan wouldn't work if I came back as Sharon. I had to borrow a body, Brady. I borrowed the most beautiful face and body I could find."

Brady gazed at Rosha's sparkling green eyes. Her shiny blond hair. Her perfect face.

No, he thought. *No!*

"Don't you think I knew what a sucker you'd be for a face and body like this?" Rosha asked, stepping closer to him. "Of course I knew! That's why I picked it—to trap you!"

Laughing insanely, Rosha stepped even closer. "And it worked!" she whispered fiercely. "It worked perfectly! You fell for me. Exactly as I knew you would. And now I've got you, Brady! Right where I want you!"

Brady jerked his arm.

Rosha's fingers gripped it like steel bands.

He couldn't get loose!

She raised her free hand and touched his face.

For a split second Brady thought she was going to kiss him.

Could she have been kidding? he wondered hopefully. *Could this whole thing be some kind of weird, crazy joke?*

She can't be Sharon, back from the dead. She can't!

Slowly, Rosha's fingers slid down his cheek.

Under his chin.

Onto his neck.

She dropped his arm. Brought her hand up to join the other one.

Her fingers wrapped around his throat. She pressed her thumbs against his windpipe.

Harder.

Brady tried to pull away. Tried to raise his arms. To shove her. Break free. Break free and run.

But he couldn't move.

Couldn't move a muscle!

Rosha's grip was fierce.

Inhuman.

Her fingers wrapped tighter. Pressed harder as she strangled him.

Strangled him.

No air! Brady's brain screamed. *No air!*

His eyes bulged.

His lungs shrieked for air.

She's killing you! his mind screamed. *Fight! Save yourself!*

The bright snow began to dim.

Darker. Darker.

I'm dead! Brady realized.

She killed me.

22

Helpless against Rosha's strength, Brady dropped to his knees in the snow.

Rosha sank with him, her hands still wrapped around his throat.

Everything faded to black.

You're dead! Brady's mind whispered frantically. *She's killed you!*

You're dead!

"That's enough, Sharon!" a voice cried out from nearby. "You're finished now!"

Incredibly, Sharon's fingers loosened from Brady's throat.

"It's over, Sharon!" the voice shouted. "It's all over for you!"

Sharon's hands dropped away. Brady pitched forward into the snow. As he shoved himself up to his knees, he looked up, gasping.

The scarred girl stood a few yards away. Her eyes glittered with rage.

Rage at Sharon.

"You've had your fun, Sharon," the scarred girl declared coldly. "Now give me back my body."

She stepped closer.

"No!" Sharon cried, springing to her feet.

"Give it back," the girl demanded.

"I'm keeping this body!" Sharon insisted. "It's mine now!"

"It's mine!" the girl shouted. She advanced another step. "You took it from me! You killed me for it!"

"And I'm going to keep it!" Sharon spun away, kicking a spray of snow into Brady's face.

Brady staggered weakly to his feet. He trembled all over. The glaring snow stabbed at his eyes. He blinked and tried to focus.

How could the scarred girl be alive? She just said she was dead! She said Sharon killed her! How could any of this be happening?

"You killed me, Sharon," the girl repeated. Her scars blazed red in the cold air. Her ruined face twisted hideously. "I was beautiful. So beautiful. I had everything to live for. And you took it all away!"

"Yes!" Sharon exclaimed.

"You didn't even know me," the girl continued. "But you killed me. You killed me and stole my beautiful body!"

Brady's throat ached. Questions whirled in his mind, but he couldn't speak.

His arms hung limply.

His legs could barely hold him upright.

Shaken and dazed, all he could do was watch as the scarred girl stalked slowly across the snow.

Stalked toward Sharon.

"I was weak for so long," the girl told Sharon. "You thought I'd stay that way forever, didn't you? But I didn't. I'm strong now."

"Strong?" Sharon sneered. "You're dead. You're nothing—nothing but a shell. A weak, hideous, disgusting shell!"

The girl shook her head. Her lips peeled back from her teeth in an ugly smile. "Not anymore," she insisted. "It took me weeks, but now I'm strong enough to take my beautiful body back."

Brady shook his head. Tried to make the voices stop. None of this made sense. This girl talked about being dead. Dead!

How could she be dead?

How could Sharon be alive?

"Did you hear me, Sharon?" the girl shouted. "I want my body back!"

"No! Never!" Sharon screamed. "I'm never going back inside that ugly, scarred body again! Never!"

With a howl of rage the scarred girl sprang through the air. She knocked Sharon to her knees.

Brady watched helplessly as she twisted her fingers in Sharon's shiny blond hair and pulled Sharon's face into the snow. "I'm taking it back!" she shouted. "I'm taking my beautiful body back!"

"Never!" Sharon threw her off and aimed a sharp kick at the girl's scarred face. "Never!" she shrieked.

The girl leaped back, then charged at Sharon again. Brady gasped as her nails clawed at Sharon's skin.

He gasped again as Sharon's fingers gouged into the scarred girl's eyes. Digging. Twisting. Shrieking, the girl drew her fist back and slammed it into Sharon's stomach.

Sharon stumbled back, her breath heaving. The girl flew at her and knocked her to the ground.

Brady wrapped his arms around himself, still trembling.

Still weak.

Too weak to do anything but watch in horror as the two girls swirled through the snow in a raging battle.

Would Sharon win?

And what would happen to him if she did?

23

I'm taking it!" the girl roared. "I'm taking my body back!" She tore at Sharon's glossy hair, ripping clumps out by the roots.

"No!" Sharon screamed. She rolled to her back, bent her legs, then kicked out with both feet at the girl's chest.

The girl sprawled backward. Sharon leaped on her.

Brady tried to yell. Nothing emerged but a croak. He swallowed painfully and tried again. "Stop!" he shouted. "You're both crazy!"

His voice was stronger this time, but it made no difference. The two girls continued to tear into each other.

Their arms and legs became a blur as they tumbled over and over, punching and kicking.

With a fierce cry the scarred girl rolled on top

of Sharon and grabbed her arm with both hands.

Brady heard a horrible ripping noise.

Sharon's arm!

The scarred girl tore Sharon's arm off at the shoulder!

Bright red blood spurted from the torn socket and splattered across the snow.

"No!" Brady cried. "Noooo!"

The girl bared her teeth in a hideous grin and grabbed for Sharon's other arm. But Sharon slithered away, then dived for the girl's leg.

The girl screamed in agony as her leg ripped loose. Sharon flung the leg across the snow.

"Nooo!" Brady screamed again. He squeezed his eyes shut and shook his head violently.

He opened his eyes in time to see another leg spinning through the air.

Another arm.

Sharon dragged herself through the snow, leaving a trail of blood. Her breath came in hoarse, ragged gasps. She wrapped her remaining arm around the scarred girl's neck.

Both of them began to pull at each other.

"Nooo!" Brady could only moan now. "Nooo!"

They pulled harder. Harder.

Brady stared in horror as their necks twisted.

Strained.

Snapped.

Their heads ripped off. Both heads; both. Mouths locked in silent screams.

Arms and legs, bodies and heads whirled through the snow.

Then began to tumble down the steep sledding hill.

Brady gazed in horror as the body parts rolled and tumbled through the snow. Rolling through the trees, bouncing through the bushes, down, down—all the way down Miller Hill.

And then vanished in the snow.

Vanished completely.

Brady heard the sound of his breathing.

Saw nothing but clean white snow, sparkling brightly in the sun.

EPILOGUE

Brady trudged along the sidewalk toward Allie's house. He'd left his car at the park yesterday, and he knew he had to dig it out.

But first, he wanted to see Allie.

He gazed up at the morning sun. Its rays were weak and didn't warm him at all. But he knew Allie would warm him up. The thought made him smile.

Along Allie's block, people shoveled their sidewalks and dug their cars out. A friend of Brady's mother waved at him across the top of her car. Then she called his name.

Brady didn't stop. He had to see Allie. He had to make everything all right with her.

Farther along the block a little kid lobbed a snowball at him. Brady saw it coming, but he didn't try to duck or move out of the way. The snowball splatted against the side of his coat. But it didn't matter to him.

Nothing mattered except Allie.

Allie's long driveway was still covered with snow. No one had shoveled yet. Brady plunged into it and staggered toward the house.

The porch and steps had been cleared. Brady climbed up and pushed the doorbell. Waited. Waited.

No one came.

She has to be here, he thought. *I need to talk to her. She has to be here!*

Shivering, Brady turned and shuffled back across the porch.

As he started down the steps, he heard a metallic scraping sound coming from the back of the house.

Snow shovel. Someone out back, shoveling the terrace.

Let it be Allie, he thought desperately as he rounded the corner of the house. *I need to see her. Let it be Allie.*

Allie stood at the bottom of the back terrace, scraping the last of the snow from the steps. She wore jeans tucked into bright blue snow boots. Yellow gloves, but no jacket. Just a heavy fisherman's sweater. Her auburn hair glowed like fire in the morning sun.

"Aren't you cold?" Brady asked.

Allie jumped. "Brady! You scared me!" she exclaimed.

"Sorry." Brady smiled at her with numb lips. "I just wondered why you didn't have a jacket on. It's cold out here. Aren't you cold?"

Shaking her head, Allie started shoveling the back walk. "I've been doing this for half an hour. I feel like I'm in a sauna." She tossed a shovelful of snow to the side and glanced at him. "You look awful, Brady. Just awful."

"I know. I didn't sleep very well," he told her.

"Maybe you should go home and go back to bed," she said. "What are you doing here, anyway?"

She's still angry, Brady thought. He couldn't blame her, but he had to try to make things right. "I, um . . ." He approached her shyly. "I came to apologize again."

Allie gazed at him silently. Her gray eyes doubtful.

"I acted really dumb," Brady continued. "I came to say I'm sorry. Real sorry."

She stared at him a moment longer. "Well. Thanks for the apology, Brady." She turned away and began to scrape up more snow.

"I mean it, Allie!" Brady declared. "I feel terrible about everything. I acted like a super jerk. I don't blame you for hating me. But I want to get back together. Can you take me back?"

"Oh, Brady." Allie sighed. "I don't know. I'm not sure."

"Please," he pleaded. "It will be different this time, I promise. Remember how it was when we first started going together?"

"Of course I do," Allie replied softly. "It was great. I thought it would stay that way,"

"I know. But it can be like that again, Allie," Brady promised. "All you have to do is take me back and everything will be the way it used to be. Everything will be perfect."

Allie sighed again and leaned on the shovel. "I just—"

"Please," Brady interrupted. "Please say yes, Allie." He shivered. Waited tensely for her answer.

After a long minute, Allie smiled. "Well, okay, Brady," she said. "Yes. Let's start all over again."

"That's great. That's so great," Brady murmured with a sigh of relief. He stepped closer and cupped her cheek in his hand.

Allie flinched and jerked her head away. "Sorry!" she exclaimed with a little laugh. "But your hand is freezing!"

"Yeah," Brady agreed. "I'm cold all over. That's something I have to talk to you about," Brady told her. "See, there's just one small problem."

Allie glanced up, a questioning expression in her gray eyes.

"You remember Rosha, don't you?" Brady asked.

Allie dropped his hands. "What's going on, Brady? I mean, I thought it was over between you and Rosha."

"Well, it is. But . . ." Brady hesitated. "There is one slight problem."

"Problem? What problem?" Allie demanded.

"I'm dead," Brady told her.

"Huh?" Allie stared at him.

"It's true," he explained. "That's why I look so bad. I died yesterday. Rosha killed me up on Miller Hill."

"Brady, stop joking!" Allie pleaded. "That's sick. That's really sick. It's not funny!"

"I'm not joking, Allie," Brady insisted. "She strangled me. Rosha strangled me. I'm dead."

"Stop it!" Allie backed up a step.

Brady reached out and took hold of her hand. "That's why I'm so cold, Allie. So cold. So cold. Because I'm dead."

"Brady, please!" Allie cried.

Brady tugged on her hand, pulling her close to him. He leaned down and kissed her lips. "You're so warm and I'm so cold."

Allie wrenched herself away. Stumbling backward, she gazed at him in horror. "Yuck! Your lips!" she shrieked. "They're so cold!"

"Take me back anyway!" Brady pleaded desperately. He staggered toward her. "Okay, Allie? Take me back even though I'm dead. Okay? Okay?"

Her eyes wide with terror, Allie opened her mouth and began to scream.

Turn the page for a peek

at Fear Street:

SECRET ADMIRER

PROLOGUE

Dear Selena,

Your name means "moon." Like the moon, you are pale, beautiful, and mysterious. Your blond hair is silvery like the moon's rays.

Everyone admires you. Everyone applauds for you.

I'm in your audience too, Selena.

Though I see you every day, you don't see me. But someday that will change.

Someday I will be the only person in your audience.

It will be just you and me, Selena.

Someday.

Someday very soon.

Yours forever,

The Sun

1

He'll never hurt you again. I promise. He'll never hurt you again." Selena Goodrich's last words were almost a whisper.

The audience began to clap. Slowly the curtain came down, closing off the stage. Then it rose again.

Selena stepped to the front of the stage, smiling as she gazed out over the audience. Accepting the cheers and applause.

She bowed deeply, her blond curls tumbling over her shoulders. Then she straightened and turned to the other actors in the cast. She joined hands with Alison Pearson and Jake Jacoby, and the line of actors—everyone in the play—bowed together. The audience leaped to its feet, cheering loudly.

All these people came to see me, Selena thought in wonder. *I belong on the stage. Finally I know where I fit in.*

The curtain sank for the final time. Selena turned to her friends. "You were both terrific," she told them.

"Thanks, Selena," Alison murmured. Alison was pretty, with emerald eyes and long, straight black hair. She smiled at Selena. "But I'll never be as good as you. You were awesome!"

"Hey—you weren't bad, Moon," Jake added, punching Selena lightly on the shoulder. Of all her friends, he was the only one who still called Selena by her childhood nickname. He loved to tease her, and he knew the nickname annoyed her. Most other people didn't even know that "Selena" meant "moon."

"You weren't so bad yourself. At least you didn't fall on your face this time," Selena replied, rolling her eyes. "Are you going to the cast party?"

Jake shrugged. "I don't know," he said. "I'm not really psyched for a party."

Even through the stage makeup, Selena could see that Jake had dark circles under his eyes. She was about to ask him if anything was wrong when the drama club director swept between them.

"Congratulations, Selena!" he called out. "Tonight's performance was excellent. I love that thing you did with the handkerchief in the last act. You surprised even me!"

"Thank you, Mr. Riordan," Selena replied with a smile.

The handsome, gray-haired teacher stepped onto a riser and shouted for attention. "I'll see all of you at my house for the party!" he called over the buzz of voices. "But before we go, I want to remind you about tryouts next week for the spring play. You'll be happy to hear that we're doing a classic—*Romeo and Juliet*."

This news was greeted with a mixture of groans and cheers.

Romeo and Juliet! Selena thought with excitement. *I'll get a chance to do Shakespeare on stage!*

She hurried to her locker, pushing through the loud, happy crowd of actors backstage.

"Yo, Selena!" Danny Morris called. "Good job! You were cool!"

"Thanks," Selena replied curtly. She pushed past the stocky blond senior. Catching the disappointment on his tanned face, she felt the tiniest pang of guilt. *Maybe I should be nicer to Danny,* she thought.

After all, we meant something to each other . . . once. A long time ago.

These days, Selena couldn't figure out why all the girls at Shadyside High found Danny so fascinating.

She still couldn't believe she'd gone out with him for as long as she did. How had she been able to stand his showing off and selfishness for six whole months?

"Trying out for the spring play?" Danny demanded, stepping in front of her to block her path.

"Of course I am." Selena sighed. She tried to move around him, but he refused to budge. "Danny, listen, I'm in kind of a hurry—"

"You'll get to play Juliet for sure," Danny persisted, ignoring her attempts to get past. "Guess which part I'm trying out for."

"The castle pest?" Selena cracked.

"Selena!"

Selena turned at the familiar voice of her best friend, Katy Jensen. Katy came hurrying over in her stagehand's black coveralls.

"Later," she told Danny as Katy approached.

"You were excellent!" Katy gushed. "Even better than last night." She gave Selena a quick hug.

"Everyone hit it perfectly tonight," Selena told her friend. "It's like it all finally came together. And everything backstage went perfectly."

Katy wiped her forehead with the back of her hand. Her short, straight black hair stood on end. Her pale, round face shone with sweat in the dim backstage lights.

"I had a problem with the lights," she commented. "Didn't you notice?"

"Not at all," Selena replied.

"One of the spots became unfocused," Katy explained. "I rushed up there as soon as I saw it." She pointed to the catwalk that stretched high above the stage.

Selena glanced up and shuddered. *How could anyone have the nerve to climb up there?* she wondered. Just the sight of the narrow metal ladder built into the wall made her feel dizzy.

But Katy never seemed to mind heights. Even when they were little kids, she had been the one to climb trees while Selena cowered on the ground.

I guess that's why Katy likes being on the stage crew, Selena thought absently. She pulled open the door of the big locker room.

It was crowded with her friends from the play. While the play was in progress, this room doubled as the girls' dressing room. "I don't know why we even bother with lockers," Katy commented. "None of them lock anyway."

Selena shrugged.

"So are you ready for your next role?" Katy asked.

"What do you mean?" Selena demanded as she exchanged grins with Alison, who was also trying to push through the crowd of students.

"Come on." Katy laughed. "You know you'll get Juliet."

"Everyone keeps saying that," Selena declared. "But it's not like there's a guarantee I'll get the part."

Katy snorted. "Yeah, well, there's no guarantee the sun will rise tomorrow. But everyone knows you're perfect for Juliet. I mean, it's the last play of the year. No one will come if you aren't the star."

"Yeah, right!" Selena rolled her eyes.

Why did Katy always have to exaggerate everything? "Anyway, it's up to Mr. Riordan," she added.

"What's up to me?" Mr. Riordan approached the girls.

"We're talking about casting for the spring play," Selena told him.

Mr. Riordan nodded. "Casting for this next play might be particularly important," he confided.

"Why?" Katy asked.

"Well, it's supposed to be a secret, but . . . I just found out that the drama coach from Northwestern University will be here," Mr. Riordan whispered.

"You're kidding!" Selena gasped. Northwestern had one of the best drama departments in the country.

"I'm serious," he told her. "Each year he visits

different schools in the area to check out the talent. This year he has chosen Shadyside High."

"Whoa!" Selena cried. "I'm applying to Northwestern. But there's no way I can go without a scholarship."

"Then this is your big chance," Mr. Riordan said with a wink. He turned and headed for the stage door. "See you girls at the party."

"You never told me you wanted to go away to college," Katy remarked.

"Well, sure I *want* to," Selena replied. "But it's only a dream. I mean, Mom doesn't even make enough money to send me to the junior college."

"If that drama coach sees you play Juliet, he'll give you the scholarship," Katy predicted.

"That would be amazing," Selena replied. "But I'll believe it when I see it."

Most of the other students had cleared out. Selena yanked open the door of her locker. Her backpack hung on the hook where she'd left it.

But leaning against the pack, she saw something new—a large bouquet, wrapped in blue-striped paper.

"What is it?" Katy asked, gazing over Selena's shoulder.

"Cool!" Selena exclaimed. "Someone left me flowers! I wonder who?"

"Open them!" Katy urged.

Selena carefully pulled out the wrapped bouquet.

She ripped the paper from the top and peered inside.

And then she gasped in open-mouthed horror.